# A Chinese Odyssey

BY

AXEL FORRESTER

FLYING
START

PRESS

First published in 2022 by Flying Start Press

A Cataloguing in Publication record for this
book is available from the British Library
Cover design by Axel Forrester

ISBN: 9781739653989

# Chapter One

July 2010   St Ives, Cornwall

I was at home, sitting in my favourite chair, thinking about my first photo assignment outside of Cornwall. I'd be away for three weeks, but it was good money. Katie would be pleased for me, wouldn't she? I'd just have to find the right way to bring it up.

Katie was working in the same room, on her laptop. Ariel came crashing through the front door. It slammed shut in the backdraft. She tossed her school bag on the floor.

'Nee HOW!' she called out at the top of her lungs, hands on hips. She then took the stairs up to her room, two at a time.

Katie scratched her nose and tucked a strand of hair behind her ear. The summer sun had lightened it already.

'Ariel? Come back here! What did you just say?'

I headed for the kitchen.

'I'll start some dinner,' I said over my shoulder, glad to disappear.

It was my night to cook.

'Hold on.' Katie stood up and went to the stairs. 'Ariel?' she called up.

'Nothing! It was nothing!' came our daughter's voice from above.

Katie fixed her eyes on me. 'What's going on?'

I raised my shoulders and dropped them again, then stared at the floorboards of our old house. Katie inherited it from her mother. Our cat, Cassandra, also inherited, was eyeing me with suspicion. She started up her low cat growling.

'Pasta? Or shall I make a big salad? It's getting warmish again, isn't it?'

'You're stalling.'

'Right. Well, I can make a lentil stew. Would you prefer that? Something hot?'

'Ariel?' She called upstairs again. 'Come down here, please.'

'I'll get started chopping—'

'Not so fast. Since when, do *you* start making dinner at 3:30?'

Katie had her arms crossed. Cassandra's tail was swishing back and forth, menacingly. Her eyes were green slits.

Ariel came tumbling down the stairs. She was practicing her rolls from gym class. Impressively, she landed on her feet.

'Ta-da!' she cried, arms out wide.

I clapped wildly.

'Stupendous! That was great! Wasn't it, honey?' I grinned at Katie. 'And no injuries!'

'Oh, the day isn't over yet.' My wife narrowed her eyes at me. 'Who's going to tell me about Nee How? I want to know – now.'

Katie was using her courtroom voice. Ariel and I both knew what that meant. No horsing

3

around. Ariel pointed to me and batted her eyelashes. I opened my mouth to say something, anything, but my daughter beat me to it.

'Dad's just helping me learn Chinese. Ni Hao. It means hello in Chinese.'

I had to admire the save. It wasn't a lie. I *was* teaching her a little of the language.

'You're learning *Chinese* in school? In Year One?' Katie asked, somewhat incredulous.

Ariel stroked Cassandra's head. Our ginger cat was big with white paws. She usually liked being petted, but today she was having none of it. She jumped off the back of the sofa and went off in a sulk.

'We learn all kinds of stuff at school.' She was my daughter all right. I liked her evasive moves. Ariel looked up at the ceiling and started dancing around. Which she was prone to do.

'You've got homework. Right?' I said, hopefully.

She stopped. 'Yes, I do.'

'Go on upstairs then and get started. I'll be up to help a bit later.'

'OK!' She turned and raced up the stairs. 'Hua bié!'

I closed my eyes.

'Well?' Katie folded her arms.

'It's amazing how fast she picks it up. Chinese! Right? I was just messing around with her.'

'Teaching her Mandarin?'

I laughed – one of those guilty, girlish laughs.

'Come on, Grant! Tell me!'

'Gosh. Katie. All right. All right. I've been waiting for the right time—'

'Now. Now's a good time. Just tell me.'

The intensity of Katie's sea-green eyes when she's after information is like that of a cobra. There is no escape. No place to hide. Every muscle in my body went rigid with tension. I put up my hands in surrender.

'Let's sit down. It's not bad. I promise. It's good news!'

'Oh, is it now?'

She folded her legs under a petite, athletic body and sank into our well-worn sofa. Katie still surfed just about every morning, no matter what the weather. It kept her in good shape. She's very strong.

'I got an email from a former colleague, about a photography gig.'

Katie raised her eyebrows.

'Oh?'

'Yes.' I sucked in my lips and then puckered them out again.

'And? Where is it?'

'Well...China.'

'China.'

'Kunming, mostly. The Yunnan province. South of Beijing.' Now I was doing the eyebrow-raising, rolling my eyes a bit. 'Can you believe it?'

'For how long?'

I folded my hands together, then unfolded them and rubbed the back of my neck.

'Three weeks.'

Katie let the words hang in the air. She didn't move.

'That's a long time.' She swallowed and shifted on the sofa. 'What kind of pictures are you expected to take?'

'Documenting. A group trip. Bunch of American teachers are going. They'll want pictures of what they do and see, and pictures of the Chinese teachers and students.'

Katie shifted in her seat.

'Why did they ask you to come? How did they know about you?'

I dropped down before her on the floor and gently put my hands on her knees.

'I told you. Someone going on the trip knew me. A former colleague. She's... a history teacher—'

Katie's eyes grew wide.

'No.' Then wider. 'Not...Charon Fields. Your old girlfriend?'

I stood up.

'It was a long time ago, Katie.'

She went into the kitchen and took out pots and pans. She banged them down on the stove. I followed her but stayed a safe distance.

Her voice was raised in that highly controlled way she has when she's really mad.

'You've been emailing your ex and you didn't TELL me?'

'I didn't want to upset you. See? You're upset!'

She slammed a cupboard door shut.

'Of course, I'm upset! You want to go away to China for three weeks with your ex-girlfriend! Are you sharing a room too?'

'No. No! Or…well, I don't *know* exactly what the sleeping arrangements will be…'

I cringed. *Shouldn't have put it like that.*

Katie pulled out another pan and dropped it to the floor with a crash. She then went upstairs, stomping all the way. I knew what was coming. She came back down a few minutes later in her wetsuit.

'I'm not hungry. Have dinner without me.'

'What should I feed Ariel?'

'Oh, whatever you feel like. You can make all kinds of decisions without *me*. Right?'

'Katie. I haven't made any decisions. We're just talking about this now. You and me.'

'You're learning Chinese! You've obviously decided you're going!'

'Oh, come on, Katie. It's a good job. Good money. I just have to document the trip. They're paying my way. I'll get £5000 for three weeks work. Come on – you should be excited. This is a good gig!'

Katie glared.

'It's great. All good, except for Charon NEE HOW Fields!'

Katie went out the front door and slammed it after her.

# Chapter Two

Katie didn't come back until it was time to put Ariel to bed. It was her night to read the story and do the honours, but I listened by the door.

'Is Daddy going to China?'

A long silence.

'Maybe. We'll see.'

'Don't you want him to go?'

A big sigh.

'Not really. Do you?'

'No...but he really wants to see China. *I'd* like to see China.'

'What do you know about it?'

'Miss Allen showed it to us on the globe. I saw some pictures too. Daddy showed me. In a magazine. It looks amazing.'

'Yes, I suppose it is, but it's a very long way from here.'

'It's on the other side of the world. But he could take pictures and bring them back and show them to us.'

'He could.'

'It will be like he's bringing us with him. He'll show us what he sees.'

'I suppose so.'

Another big sigh from Katie.

'And we can have fun too. The two of us. And Cassandra. It will be all girls in the house.'

'That's true. You think we can manage on our own?'

'Course we can. Girl power!'

I took a step back, relieved. They'd be fine. Now it was going to be up to me not to screw things up.

Making up with Katie that night was lovely. In the morning, with my arms around her, I had a sudden pang of regret. Three weeks was a very

11

long time to be away. We'd not been apart that long ever before.

Once I'd arrived at Katie's house, six years ago, from California, I stayed. St Ives was the last stop on my walking tour of Cornwall. She helped me find a way to stay and it wasn't long before I understood that *Katie* was my home.

And it was here, in St Ives, that I got my first job as a photographer. Being a photographer was what I'd wanted to do my whole life, but this was where I found the courage to actually do it. This was the place where everything changed for me, where I understood who I was.

'Maybe I shouldn't go,' I whispered. 'I already have work here.'

Katie stirred from sleep.

'Hmmm?'

'The job. Maybe I should give it a pass. It *is* far and a long time to be away.'

Katie sat up and pulled a pillow to her chest. The sunlight was coming through the window and pooling at the foot of our bed. Her lovely eyes were staring at me, perplexed.

'You're a photographer. This is a job. You have to go.'

I sighed and pulled her close.

'But I don't want to leave.'

She turned my chin to her and kissed me deeply and I was lost in her again. Moving my hands through her hair and down her body, I still couldn't quite believe she was my wife. How had I been so lucky? Katie drew back.

'The thing is...we have plans now. Girly plans. Ariel and I.'

'Girly plans?' I got up from the bed and put my hands on my hips. 'Are you setting up some kind of female, witchy, mermaid, power convergence portal?'

'I can neither confirm nor deny such a plan.'

'Uh, huh. Is Cassandra involved?'

'Of course.'

'And you want me out of the house?'

'Well, you wouldn't want to be around.'

'Are you shoving me out the door to China then?'

'For your own good, luv. However, this is not a free ticket to carouse with the she-demon Charon.'

'I understand. There will be no carousing. *Especially* with the she-demon.'

13

Katie laughed.

'I've told Ariel she can invite her girlfriends. Mermaid party. We're making popcorn and cupcakes.'

'And I'm going to miss all the fun?'

'Well, you'll be having fun in China.'

I sighed.

'It's a bit dangerous, you know.'

'Oh? You didn't tell me that.'

'I didn't know. I just got the medical packet yesterday. It's huge. There's malaria there. And THE PLAGUE!'

Katie stood up now and concern was spreading across her face.

'And these teachers are going?'

'We all have to take malaria medicine and it says on the packet it isn't likely we'll get the plague, but it's possible.'

'My goodness.' Katie took a deep breath in and then let it out. She looked calm. 'This makes it...a real adventure then.'

I didn't say what I was thinking – that the plague was nothing compared to Charon. She was the most dangerous element of the trip. I feared her diabolical powers.

'So, you think I should risk it?'

Katie kissed my nose.

'There are risks to everything worth doing. But you can manage it. You're an adventurer. This is a big chance for you.'

'You think I'll be, OK?'

'I know you will. We're constructing the portal to bring you back safe. The hero always returns.'

At that moment, I loved Katie even more, if that was possible. She thought me an adventurer and was counting on me to come back. I was not going to let her and Ariel down.

The emails were now flying back and forth between St Ives and Los Angeles. I was determined to keep my tone business-like with Charon. She had been so bossy in our relationship. Always thought me incapable of anything. I never quite understood why it lasted so long. Nine years. I suppose it was because we worked at the same school. It was convenient. Charon always tried to steer us toward marriage, but I resisted. Thank goodness.

After my hiking trip around Cornwall, I announced to friends and family I was not returning to North Hollywood. I was staying in St Ives. Charon was particularly incensed and told me I had lost my mind. Our relationship thus at an end, I didn't expect to hear from her ever again.

It was a surprise when I got the email from her a few weeks earlier. Charon was still teaching US history at the school where we both had worked. She was doing some sort of video project about women in China.

'This is my time, Grant. My documentary is going to be a-mazing.' Even over the phone, I could imagine Charon, flicking her ash blonde hair over her shoulder as she made this statement. She did this often, like a nervous tick. Because she spent a fortune on her hair, she liked to show it off.

'I'm sure it will be.'

'Oh, and I'm married now.'

That stopped me. It was hard to imagine Charon married.

'That's...great!' I felt my whole body relax in relief. She wasn't after me anymore. 'Who's the lucky man?'

'Todd. With two Ds. He teaches volleyball. At another school. It's always a mistake to date someone in your place of work.'

That stopped me too.

'Right. So, uh, Charon. I wanted to thank you for recommending me for this gig. I'm looking forward to going.'

'Grant?'

'Yes?'

'Listen very carefully. I'm risking my reputation by recommending you for this job. So, don't you DARE make me regret it!'

'No. I won't. You won't regret it.'

'It was a favour. Because of old times.'

'I appreciate it.'

'Do NOT screw this up. I'm warning you.'


The day arrived. My bags were packed. This time I made sure to have the whistle that I didn't bring when I hiked in Cornwall. I wanted to return alive to Katie and Ariel and I tried to get *everything* on the list. We were limited to one bag and a carry-on, which had to be my camera bag.

'My phone won't work in China,' I said. 'Wrong network. I'll try to email to stay in touch, but not sure how I'll do it yet.'

'You'll find a way.' Katie said. She had confidence in me.

'I will.'

'Got your malaria meds?'

'Check!'

'Rain poncho?' asked Ariel.

'Check!'

Cassandra hissed.

'Check!'

'Taxi's here,' Katie said, after glancing out the window.

Ariel threw her arms around me and hugged. Tightly.

'Love you, Daddy. Come home safe.'

'I will, Pumpkin. I love you too. Take care of Mummy.'

Katie pried her off me and kissed me with a chaste, Mummy kiss, but her eyes were X-rated. *My* eyes returned the sentiment. *I'm going to miss the hell out of you.*

'Hua bié!' Ariel cried, *her* eyes filling with tears.

'Hua bié, sweetie. Don't worry. I'll be back before you know it.'

I picked up my bags and headed for the door, not quite believing I was doing this. Cassandra was sending me her warnings of doom, both telepathically and in the form of cryptic mewling. *'I know, I know,'* I said back to her, telepathically. *'I'm taking foolish chances. What am I doing, Cassandra?'* *'I don't know,'* she answered. *'You're a fool.'*

# Chapter Three

From St. Ives, I took a train to London, a journey of over seven hours, and spent the night near Heathrow. Leaving London, I would be flying to Amsterdam for two hours, making a connection there to Shanghai, an eleven-hour flight, then I had to wait five hours for a two-hour flight to Beijing. Once there, I had to make a connecting flight to Kunming, three and a half hours. A total of around nineteen hours flying, seven hours on a train, and six hours waiting in airports. Still, at least I had one of the two nights I was travelling in a hotel. The teachers were flying from LA to Vancouver and then to Beijing. Something like twenty-eight hours of flying. Brutal.

Charon had advised me before I left to have lots of Starbucks coffee in the various airports before I reached China.

'Why?' I asked.

'You won't see anything that even *resembles* coffee for three weeks.'

'What do you mean?'

'Our host, Mr Anderson, told me this. He's the American in charge of teacher groups in Kunming. He knows these things. They do not have food in this part of China, as we know it, Grant.'

'Well, all right, but no coffee? Really?'

'We're going south of Beijing, to the *country*. They do things the old way there. It's very different. There's no coffee, milk, cheese, pizza, hamburgers, bread of any kind...there will be nothing you would normally eat. Nothing. EVERYTHING they put in their *mouths* is different from what we eat.'

'Well...that's part of the adventure of travel, right?'

'This is seriously different. After two weeks, we'll be going to Beijing, where there's a more civilized way of life. They have MacDonald's there, but we'll have no such thing in Kunming. I'm just warning you, all right, toots?'

I hated it when she called me that.

'All right. What about drinking the water?'

'Jesus! Grant! Why do you think they drink so much tea? They boil EVERYTHING and we must too. Did you not read the medical packet?'

'Right. Right. Sorry. I forgot. Only bottled water or canned drinks. Or tea.'

I could hear her roll her eyes at me over the phone.

'If you get malaria – I swear to God, Grant, I'll kill you. Do NOT embarrass me.'


I had so much Starbucks coffee at the airport that I couldn't sleep on any of the flights, and I had to get up constantly to visit the bathroom. At least this got me walking around the cabin a lot, which is supposedly good for leg circulation on long trips on airplanes. I had time to think as I paced up and down the aisles. I thought of the life I had left behind, that of a teacher at the swanky high school in North Hollywood. I suppose it was the money that kept me chained there, teaching photography, but it was also my family's approval. They were all teachers. They thought that teaching was the only real thing worth doing.

Once on the ground, while waiting for my last two flights, I dreaded the prospect of being around teachers again – the schedules, the planning, the competition – always trying to outdo one another. Charon was a pro at this. It had been part of the trouble in our relationship. She worked hard to be number one. In her view, my lack of interest in competing with her was a major character flaw.

I was shattered when I finally landed in Kunming. After emerging from customs, inspections, passport control and collecting my luggage, I came, at long last, to the reception area. It felt like I had entered a carnival. The noise hurt my ears. I had a splitting headache and it seemed like everyone was screaming at me. I could not understand what was being said.

It all seemed like Chinese to me because...it *was* Chinese. Even with my crash Internet course in Mandarin, I did not understand one word of it.

There was a sea of very short men in black suits waving crudely handwritten signs with English names on them. Ah. I had to pay attention here. Charon said someone would be picking me up at the airport and taking me to the hotel.

Only one man was not shouting. In fact, he looked relaxed. Even bored. He held up his sign with one hand, apparently happy to let the sign do the talking. GRANT DECKER. It took a moment for my brain to turn over and recognise my name. That was me! I came up to him and waved. He looked me up and down. His face did not change. The boredom remained. It was fixed there on his face as if painted on. He turned and raised his hand in the air – the international signal for 'follow me.'

Once I was sitting in the back seat of a very old, beat-up Toyota, it became crystal clear to me how vulnerable I was. I was carrying an expensive digital camera, my new Nikon D70, I had about two thousand Yuan in my wallet, my passport, and the address of the hotel on a card. I took it out to show the driver, but we were off like a shot. He apparently already knew where we were going. He had my name. From Charon. This was part of her plan. He wasn't some random guy, kidnapping me, right?

As we drove along, I noticed flocks of people on black bicycles on either side of the car. Hundreds of them. And I didn't see any sign of a road. No tarmac. No traffic signals. Just clouds of dust all around us. There were jerky stops, starts, and near misses with other cars crossing our path.

And no seatbelts. I found myself gripping the back of the driver's seat, holding on for dear life as we zipped right, then left. This guy was making it up as he went along! Suddenly, he braked hard, throwing me forwards and then back. I realised I was riding in a death trap with a maniac.

After what seemed like an eternity, we came to a stop in front of a western-style hotel. I leapt out of the car, hugely relieved to be alive, but had to wait as my 'driver' got out of the vehicle, opened the trunk, and stood by, watching me haul the heavy suitcase out on my own. I was unsure if I was supposed to pay him or not, but he got back in the car and sped off.

I stared at the hotel sign in Chinese, and then at my card. The name looked the same. I guessed this was it. After staggering up the stairs, I went through the double glass doors and into the lobby.

It was a windowless room with high ceilings and a huge crystal chandelier. There was faded striped wallpaper, and a man with his head down at the reception desk.

Dragging my bag behind me, I approached him, the squeaking wheels sounding as tired as I felt.

'About time!'

I turned toward the sound of that grating, familiar voice. It was Charon, sitting on a Queen Anne chair – legs crossed, skirt hiked up almost to her hips, wearing five-inch red heels, a magazine on her lap.

'Charon!'

I started to sit down on a chair next to hers, but she stood up.

'Don't sit down. Did you get any sleep last night?'

'No.'

'Come with me. I'll show you to your room. You just have time to take a quick nap before our orientation meeting.'

We walked to the reception desk where the man lifted his head.

'This is Mr Decker,' she said. 'Number 39.'

The man reached for a plastic disk with the number 39 on it and handed it to me.

'No key?' I asked. The man just stared at me. Then he looked to Charon.

'I'll explain later,' she said, in a low voice. 'Just follow me.'

We walked to the elevator and went inside the open doors. Charon pressed the third button up from the bottom.

'Take note. You're on the third floor. You didn't get a key because everyone here has a job and having the key is the job of the key girls.'

'Key girls. That sounds a bit sexist.'

Charon shot me a look.

'They do things differently here, toots. Pay attention. You're not in Kansas anymore. This

27

hotel is owned by the Yunnan University, our host.' She stopped and faced me. 'Our first meeting is in two hours. After that, we'll be having dinner here at the hotel. We're having all our meals together. Part of the package. As I told you.'

'Oh. Really? Every meal?'

'We're on a very tight schedule. You have to keep up. Here's a printout of the activities. As I said in my email, you won't have Internet here at the hotel. And American cell phones don't work on China's network. The hotel won't allow long distance calls, either.'

'So, there's no way to contact my wife?'

'Not easily, no.'

'I guess I'll have to find some kind of Internet café somewhere.'

'Yeah, good luck with that. Maybe you'll find something if you get some free time, but I doubt you will. She can live without you for a few weeks. Now go and have a nap.'

Charon stepped up to me and put out both arms. It took me a moment to realise she was offering a parting hug. I bent down and put my arms around her, awkwardly.

'Welcome to China, Grant.'

She did not hug back. Charon had intimacy issues. She just submitted to hugs, like something annoying that often messed up her hair. I wondered how Todd with two Ds was managing it.

# Chapter Four

Dinner was held in a private dining room in the hotel. Around a circular table, there were nine other participants – teachers, mostly from the US. Our leader, Mr Guy Anderson, worked for the university in Kunming and was an American.

The orientation was an hour long; we were introduced us to each other and to our leader, the man who would negotiate all the protocols on this trip. You did not make a move in China without advanced planning, paperwork and protocols. If you did not do exactly as you were told, you would find yourself on a plane back to wherever you came from. I could already sense we were being handled like dynamite. Explosive Westerners.

Guy started banging on his cheap hotel glass with a chopstick. No other cutlery was on offer. We were expected to sink or swim here with these eating utensils. Plastic chopsticks don't make much noise on glass. He cleared his throat and it sounded like there was considerable phlegm. I thought he was choking, but afterwards, he snapped to attention, the picture of health.

'Ni Hao, everyone!' He had his arms spread wide like a ringmaster. 'Here we are at our first meal together!' A toothy smile. 'Welcome.' His accent sounded Midwestern. 'Enjoying the food?' A murmur of satisfaction around the table.

So far, the food looked very much like the Chinese food back in America – egg fried rice, sweet and sour pork, ginger beef. There were even fortune cookies. Charon was sitting next to me and whispered in my ear.

'Eat up. This is your last normal meal.'

'Tomorrow morning,' continued Guy, 'we meet on the roof of the hotel. We're going to have a lesson in Tai Chi!'

There were six women in the group. Charon and Hetty were from North Hollywood School of Art and Science, and the four female elementary school teachers were from Iowa. Ellen and Marie looked like sisters. Both were short and slim, with blunt reddish blonde haircuts that grazed their jawlines. They wore the same style of eyeglasses with squared-off black plastic frames. Katheryn and Susie were plump, with big hair. A tribe of their own. They did not look pleased at the announcement of exercise.

Of the two male teachers, one was Japanese. Mr Ogawa. What he was doing here, I could not guess. The other was a young elementary school teacher from Detroit, named Ed. He was rubbing his hands together and grinning like an idiot.

Susie raised her beefy hand and Mr Anderson called on her.

'Yes?'

'Is it safe to exercise on the roof of the hotel?'

He cast an appraising eye on the rotund Susie and paused.

'It is strictly voluntary. We'll be done by eight. At nine, we'll meet in the hotel lobby. We'll be walking from there to our breakfast spot. You're in for a real treat!'

Susie and Katheryn exchanged wary glances.

At seven the next morning, I was on the roof. It was miserably hot, and I was wearing shorts, running shoes and a t-shirt. The instructor was a venerable old Chinese gentleman who looked peaceful, standing there in a relaxed position with his hands behind his back. He surveyed us as we stood in rows before him like a general inspecting his troops.

Charon had her hair in a high ponytail pulling her face so tight it looked like she'd had a face-lift. She was wearing shorts that showed her very fit body and was she was in full makeup. Her armour. Chatting to her pal, Hetty, she stopped every now and then to sip what I assumed was pre-boiled water from her personal pink thermos. She cast a glance my way and nodded, as if mildly pleased to see me, but then screwed the cap back on her bottle and marched over to me.

'What are you doing?'

'Hi, Charon.'

'Grant! Where is your camera?'

'Can't do Tai Chi with a camera.'

'No, you can't. So, where is your camera? You are supposed to be photographing the *group* doing everything, including Tai Chi.'

'Oh? I wasn't aware—'

'You're on duty. This is your job.'

Guy was introducing the Tai Chi instructor as I slipped back downstairs to get my camera. It seemed I was to be a walking surveillance machine. This was not my idea of a photography assignment. I was already hating this gig. But I was here now, and I'd just have to make the best of it.

I took my time getting back, but when I did, the mood on the roof was decidedly changed. Eyes were wide. Necks were stiff. Everyone was pushing air in front of them with legs apart, knees bent. Susie was gone. Walking around the perimeter, I suddenly understood why. The roof was bouncing slightly as I walked. This made me stop and wonder about the weight limits. There were loose tiles everywhere.

From the hotel roof I could see long lines of dilapidated apartment buildings with little gardens around them and washing strung across every balcony and patio. The one place where no one was hanging out was the rooftop of any building. It suddenly seemed unwise to be here. I took a few shots of people as they did Tai Chi and raised my portrait lens to Charon who was glaring at me.

I snapped a few pictures of Mr Tai Chi, our leader, Guy, and Ed who grinned obnoxiously through it all, apparently unaware that he was meant to be looking seriously out into the middle distance while doing this. I could tell Ed was going to be the poster child for the trip. The eternal optimist.

When class was over, Katheryn bolted for the stairs. Ellen and Marie, who weighed next to nothing combined, giggled nervously. Mr Ogawa was bored. Charon and Hetty were red with exertion.

Later, when we met up again, we were taken to some local food stalls outside the hotel. Guy gathered us around in a circle, like a coach talking to his team.

'Here in Kunming, free enterprise is very much alive and well. Business is everywhere, but not like what you are used to in the good old U.S. of A. We're going to have breakfast at a restaurant that is quite popular. The food's typical of what people here eat in the morning.'

'Is it *safe* to eat the food?' Katheryn asked.

'Good question! It's safe because I've personally vetted the places where we'll be eating together and because everything is boiled, just like the water brought to you this morning in those thermoses, by the key girls. Did you all remember to use only the boiled water to brush your teeth?'

Sober nodding all around.

'And your malaria meds. Is everyone still taking them? Every day? Don't forget. Good. Follow me.'

We fell into line behind Guy through a crowded marketplace. The sun was peeking between long rows of tiny open-air kitchens, consisting of a few hotplates, huge, ancient-looking pots, battered and well-worn, with steam billowing out of them. Guy stopped and spread his hands, indicating we had arrived.

I looked around but could only see what looked like doll furniture, a few tiny handmade wooden tables and chairs with seats only about a foot off the ground. To my amazement, there was a whole family sitting around one of these tables, neatly tucked in. We looked like giants in comparison. I squeezed into the Lilliputian chairs, but my knees came up almost to my chin, and I had to sit sideways at the table. Charon and Hetty joined me, and had to hold their purses in their laps. They were not about to put their expensive bags on the dirt floor.

Guy astonished us all when Chinese came flying out of his mouth, at speed, to a grinning man with a dirty white apron wrapped around him a few times.

'Did you just order for us?' Susie asked.

'Yes. Because I know what's good here. And...what's safe to eat.'

Katheryn blinked at Susie.

Minutes later, we were brought bowls of hot soup with thick rice noodles, mushrooms, and things I didn't recognise.

'There's a bug in mine!' shrieked Marie. All heads swivelled toward her.

'No,' Guy said, teeth showing in a big smile. 'That's a cricket. An excellent source of protein and really quite tasty. Try it. Pick up your bowl like this, and use the chopsticks to push things down. This broth is the best in Kunming. Go ahead. Try it!'

Marie glanced at Ellen and studied her soup, but made no attempt to do as Guy suggested.

'Oh! It's fabulous!' Ed cried out. He was sitting with Mr Ogawa and Guy. Charon, not to be outdone by a Millennial, took up her bowl and tried it. She shrugged, but did not complain. A good sign.

There were other murmurs of approval coming from the tables, but Susie and Katheryn just crossed their arms and scowled. Apparently, they were prepared to miss a meal rather than eat crickets.

As I reached for my camera bag, Guy stood up from his tiny chair and in one step he was squatting between me and Charon. He put an arm around each of us.

'I'm afraid I must ask you not to take any photographs here. And actually, no photos of any kind except those that have been approved in advance.'

'What do you mean?' laughed Charon with a touch of nervousness in her voice.

'The government will not allow it. A group shot at the university, with some of the classes, is fine. Also, at the farewell dinner at the hotel in Beijing, but that's it. No candid shots from Grant here. It would be seen as...well...spying.'

'Spying!' Now Charon was turning red. I could see it. Starting at her neck.

'But you said to bring a photographer!'

'Yes! And you did! I'm sure he will take excellent pictures of the group at the university and the farewell dinner.'

'But surely there are tourists taking photographs all over the place!'

'Yes. And you and your companions can take pictures of tourist attractions, just like tourists can, when we are out on a pre-approved sight-seeing trip. That's fine. But your official photographer, Grant here, is a guest of the government and will have to follow the rules for our group. He has to stick with group photos of approved people and activities. I'm sure you don't want to antagonise my relationship with my employers or the government. Right?'

Charon bared her teeth as only Charon can, in a way that was both smiling and threatening.

'Good!' said Guy. 'Then we understand one another. I'm sure Grant doesn't want me to have to confiscate his nice camera. He would not get it back. Ever.'

Now my eyes were as big as saucers. I pulled my camera bag tighter to my chest.

'I get it, Guy,' I said. 'Only group shots at the university events and the dinner at the hotel.'

'I like this man, Charon. He's a fast learner.' Guy stood up to make an announcement to the whole group. 'We'll be visiting many fine tourist attractions over the next two weeks and you may buy photos at all these destinations or take some of your own, but please check with me to be sure it's allowed. The Chinese like their privacy. If you don't have a release, then don't take pictures of people you don't know. Your camera may be confiscated. Is that clear?'

Every face, except for Mr Ogawa, was frozen in terror.

'When you have some free time, you might want to walk around a little and explore the area around the hotel. That's allowed, as long as you don't go alone. Go in pairs or small groups.'

'Without a guide?' Ellen asked.

'What if we get sick?' Katheryn's voice cracked.

'We can't even speak the language!' screamed Hetty, who I thought was the brave one in the group.

Then I understood. Guy was letting it sink in that we were totally dependent on him.

He smiled at Charon and me, and got everyone on their feet for the next destination, which was the marketplace. It didn't look like I was going to get to a computer on my own anytime soon. An email to my wife would just have to wait a while longer.

As we walked along the crowded pavement, we noticed tiny shops facing the road. They were eight or ten feet across. A bookshop. An appliance store. To my astonishment, there was even an auto body repair shop, spilling out into the street. A female auto mechanic was under a car with a wrench.

'Will you look at that!' Charon said, pointing to the woman.

'Free enterprise,' called Guy over his shoulder. 'From selling potatoes cooked in an oil drum to fixing cars. Everyone has assigned jobs, but they can also open their own business in their free time. They can earn their own money. The economy is growing!'

We walked and walked, turning this way and that until we came to a large square with hundreds of people selling food in baskets made of both natural fibres and plastic, laid out on cloth on the ground or on small tables.

Spiky green and yellow fruits looked like they were from Mars. Even stranger were the rambutans, red and furry, the size of golf balls. One was cracked open to show a smooth, hard, yellow centre.

'Bayberries!' Guy shouted. 'Very good for you.' He picked up the bowl of bright red, textured fruit and passed it around to us. 'It's something like a cross between a strawberry and a pomegranate.' He reached in his pocket and dropped a few coins into the waiting hands of the seller. Then he pulled a string bag out of his pocket and placed the bunch of berries into it. 'This is how you shop. It isn't far from the hotel. You can come try it when you have free time.'

'But when will that be? I don't see any free time on the schedule,' Ellen said.

'We'll see how things go. You might have some later.'

The itinerary was quite packed. In the two weeks we were in Kunming, we would see a zoo, climb Xishan Mountain, visit the Great Wall, attend an Opera, talk with a monk in a monastery, take a day trip to Dali, and attend classes at the university in calligraphy, poetry, Chinese history and, of course, we would be observing Chinese art classes at local schools. Free time did not look like it would fit in. I wondered when I would find some place to email Katie. She must be wondering if I made it. I didn't want her to worry.

As we continued to walk through the market, I noticed people on bicycles in the road carrying every conceivable kind of load. Huge bags were tied to their heads. One guy was balancing furniture on a three wheeled bike. There was a large chest of drawers on it. Whole families were riding one bicycle. A man in a suit was pedalling away, with his wife, also dressed up and wearing heels, perched on the handlebars. In her lap was a child. No helmets.

Another strange sight was people walking along, in business dress, each with a pigeon in their pocket.

'What's going on with the pigeons?' I asked Guy.

'That's lunch. Fresh from the market. The vast majority of people go home for lunch. Even the school kids. And they stop by the market to get something fresh because very few homes have a refrigerator.'

'Why is that?'

'Not enough electricity in this part of China. It's rationed here. You get lights or a fridge, but not both. Even restaurants can't have it. Did you notice the goats tied up by that restaurant back there?'

'Yeah?'

'They have goat on the menu on Wednesdays.'

'They kill it right there?' cried Marie, horror-stricken.

'Yes. And they keep fish in a tank too, for the same reason. Has to be fresh.'

When we turned another corner, we were suddenly on a narrow street where everyone was selling tobacco and wearing dark blue outfits. Mao suits. I was already mourning all the lost opportunities to take amazing pictures when Charon pulled my sleeve and stepped close.

'I had no idea Guy was going to do this, Grant. You have to believe me. This is not my fault. I can't believe this picture policy!'

'Yeah, it's pretty weird, but I'm going to do what he says. I don't want my camera taken. I need it to earn my living with it. I have mouths to feed.'

'What?' Charon stepped closer. Her jaw dropped. 'You've got...kids?'

Uh oh. I had neglected to mention this.

'One. A daughter. Ariel.'

In a lightning move she punched me in the stomach. I doubled over.

'OW!'

'Why didn't you tell me you had a kid!'

Pulling myself back to a standing position, I took her by the arm.

'Let's not get too far behind the others. I don't want to be lost in China.'

We caught up with the group and everyone turned to see us standing there together.

'You all right, Charon?' Guy asked.

'Fine!'

We all watched as Charon flicked her hair, composed herself and made a point of not looking at me. Then her eyes locked on to something and we all followed her stare. A man was butchering a cow in the middle of the road, along with a woman, who had blood up to her elbows and a baby strapped on her back. Flies were swarming around this little butchering family scene, but even stranger was the fact that the man was talking on a cell phone while he was doing this.

My hands moved to my camera, but stopped, paralysed by what might happen if Guy Anderson saw me taking the best picture of my life. I waited. When his head was turned, I pressed the button.

# Chapter Five

The next day we were bussed over to the Yunnan University, which appeared to be about the same vintage as the hotel and in a similar state of disrepair. However shabby it was, though, it was the seat of Guy's power and commanded respect. Suits and ties were worn. Everyone bowed and smiled with that friendly, slightly awkward mask that people wear when they know there is no possibility of understanding the other's language.

During the introductions, Guy's eyes – and the eyes of his superiors – appeared dead-looking. He snapped his fingers at me, indicating this was my moment, and got everyone together for our first group photo. It was going to be busy today.

We all gathered in a lecture hall to hear a speech from the President of the University, translated by an interpreter. It was just as boring in translation as I'm sure it was in the original language.

My mind floated back to the speeches I'd heard from other administrators at the school where I taught photography, North Hollywood School of Art and Science. I had to pinch myself to believe I wasn't back there anymore. It was now 2010 and I was married to Katie. We had a daughter. We lived by the sea in St Ives in Cornwall. I was living my dream of being a photographer and having the life I wanted. And in this moment, I was on assignment in China. The freakish part was that I wasn't allowed to take interesting pictures! Yeah. That part was the nightmare. Like dreams where you were constantly running after a bus you would never catch, or flying but then suddenly crashing.

Charon disrupted my daydreaming with a sharp elbow to the ribs – another reminder of my past life with her.

'We gotta talk,' she whispered. Her voice strained.

'Oh? When do you suggest we do that? There's no free time.'

'The shopping centre trip. At three.'

'We're going shopping?'

'It's on the schedule! Do you not *read*?'

'How will we manage to talk alone there?'

'We have 30 minutes of free shopping. We'll find a place to talk.'

'Fine. I have to go take more pictures now.'

I left her there, annoyed that I was making plans to talk with Charon, but couldn't be spared the time to find a place to email my wife. I got nice shots of Ellen and Marie standing next to a famous Chinese poet who, we were told by Guy, still had the tattoos from his incarceration during the Cultural Revolution. He spent ten years in jail just for being a poet. He did not smile, but stood there stoically in dark robes, between Ellen and Marie, as I took their picture. These teachers from America were wearing tennis whites and grinning like Cheshire cats.

'We're getting a copy of these pictures, right Grant?' asked Marie.

'Oh, sure. I think so. Guy will have them. You can ask him.'

I got some good shots of Charon and Hetty taking notes from an interpreter who was giving a Chinese history lesson. He talked about the 56 nationalities of Chinese people, each with their own distinctive culture, dress, foods and language. Dr Sòng, a man about my age, forty or so, was also lecturing about a small ethnic minority living nearby, the Mosuo people. It was a matriarchal culture. I noticed Charon's reaction when she heard this. She whispered something to Hetty.

I got pictures of Susie learning to paint a heron with a calligraphy brush and black ink. Cultural exchange was happening all right, within the boundaries set by Guy. I wondered if we would ever meet someone with opinions not shared by the Chinese government. They were attempting to control the Internet and how people used it. All computers, even personal ones, were registered with the police, who could seize them at any time and search them. If *anything* contrary to government guidelines was found, there would be severe consequences. No wonder these Internet places were scarce.

At three, we were deposited on the steps of the local shopping centre. Guy gathered us around.

'We don't have long here. Only about thirty minutes, but I wanted you to see this. It's a department store much like any you would find in the West. China has its own brands of every gadget you can imagine – computers, cell phones, cameras, food processors, everything. And oh, yes. There is a Chinese typewriter! With about 2,000 characters on it. It's huge. Don't miss it. Now, off you go. Oh, and like I said before, they ration electricity. So, you will have the unusual experience of shopping by candlelight and having your purchases added up on an abacus. Have fun now, but be back on the bus by 3:30. No later!'

'Come on!' Charon cried, grabbing my sleeve, and we were off. Everyone else ran too. We were suddenly a bunch of mad bargain hunters on a tight schedule. We entered the store and it did indeed look like Saks Fifth Avenue or Bloomingdales, only it looked like a restaurant too, because of the candles throwing shadows everywhere.

Charon and I were soon standing before a group of mannequins. A lot of them. Maybe twelve or fourteen standing in a row. They were six feet tall and had blonde hair – quite a contrast to the little old Chinese lady walking past us.

'OK, I have a confession,' Charon said. 'I haven't been entirely honest with you about why you were chosen for this job.'

'What was the real reason?'

She flipped her hair. So far, so Charon.

'Well...I arranged to interview these two Chinese women for my documentary. Another lady I met online introduced us. These ladies are going to meet me next week and let me record them talking about their lives in China.'

'That sounds good.'

'Yeah. But, well, it has to be in a *private* space for the meeting. This isn't on the schedule. It isn't... officially...sanctioned by the government or Guy. These women are going to tell me what they really think. So, I arranged for them to come on our last day here to the hotel. In the afternoon.'

'That sounds a bit risky, Charon.'

'They're coming to room 39.'

'That's my room.'

'Yeah.'

'Well, if you really need to use it, I can go somewhere else.'

'No, Grant. The thing is, I need *you* to keep watch at the door. If Guy or anybody comes in, these ladies could get in trouble. We all could.'

'We? This is *your* project. Not mine.'

'It's going to be amazing. The older woman has memories about the cultural revolution.'

'Yes, but...'

'And the other lady had twins and had to separate from her husband so they could each raise one child. Isn't that heart breaking?'

'It is. Listen. This is very brave of you. Very impressive. But it doesn't seem like a good idea to piss off the Chinese government. Interesting as I'm sure it will be, if you get caught, bad things could happen. I'm not going to be involved. I can't be.'

Charon laughed. It was one of her fake laughs.

'Oh, Grant. You are *such* a worry wart. No one will even know. These women won't tell. I won't tell. You won't tell. It'll be fine. But I need to know I can count on you.'

I took a deep breath. I was suddenly feeling ill. She wasn't listening to me.

'Charon!' A pigeon was startled and flew above out heads. I brought my voice down again. 'This is a dangerous idea. It's dangerous for you, for me, and these women. I can't end up in a Chinese prison because of your documentary!'

'I know! I know! But listen. It will all be fine. Just a little party. If we get caught, I told these women to pretend to be call girls you had sent up to the room.'

'What? This is your back up plan? Call girls?'

'Yeah. Brilliant, eh, toots? They agreed. Even the old lady, which was kind of cool of her.'

'An old lady call girl.' I smacked my head. 'This is beyond impossible. I'm not doing it. I'm NOT.'

'But you owe me, Grant.'

'I what?'

'You know you do.'

'I know no such thing. How is it that I owe you?'

Charon lowered her shoulders. Her bottom lip protruded. Tears fell from her eyes. *Oh, no. Not the tears of Charon.*

'You know...all I ever wanted was to have your child.'

'What???'

My knees buckled.

'But it wasn't meant to be, I guess. You had a child with someone else. But this documentary? *This* is my baby, Grant. It will have to do, won't it? I didn't want to do it this way, but it was the only way I could think of. Hetty is going to be my alibi and say I was with her the whole time in our room, but I need *you* Grant, watching the door of Room 39. If you don't do this, I can't make my documentary. It will be twice that you've denied me what I want most. You have to help me. You have to!'

I was angry. So angry that I whirled around and my backpack caught one of the mannequins, which teetered on two spindly legs with six-inch heels. To my horror, that mannequin leaned on to the next mannequin, who leaned on to the next and so on, until all of them went down domino style, crashing to the marble floor in an ear-splitting KA BOOM!

We ran for the door, dashed down the steps, and leapt onto the waiting bus without looking behind us.

'Points for Grant and Charon!' yelled Katheryn. 'Five points for being late!'

# Chapter Six

More days passed in Kunming and I was no nearer to finding a place to email my wife. I hoped she assumed I was all right. There was nothing I could do about it. I asked Guy a few times if I could email my wife or even just use a phone. I'd be glad to pay him. He just looked at me blankly, and ignored me. Charon was no help either. I'd just have to follow along with the program and take pictures as directed.

We experienced a shortened version of a Chinese Opera. For two hours, there was screeching and yelling of a kind that made us cover our ears. I could not imagine a regular version, which, Guy told us, was fourteen hours long.

He said that people came prepared to cook their own food and camp out, and that it was very noisy as people chatted and talked loudly among themselves. The opera singers had to find ways to get their attention and the screeching was part of that. Drama. Costumes. Spectacle. Like TV, I guess. I tried to slip out, but Guy was guarding the door.

During this period, we also went to different primary schools to understand more about how the Chinese teach art. Children attended school six days a week, from about eight in the morning until six in the evening. They all went home for a two-hour lunch, but this still struck me as a long time to be in school. Forty-eight hours a week!

Guy explained that children go to school to the age of fourteen, and are then tested. Only the top four percent go on to further education. No wonder they worked hard. Their future was decided at fourteen. It was either key girl, or go on to higher education like Dr Sòng.

With this information, I had a better understanding of why Chinese children in the US were expected by their parents to work long hours and perform well. Families had been practicing getting good grades for generations. The benefits were clear to them.

I also understood now why there were lots of mannequins together in the department stores. Class sizes were 50. Kids grew up in big groups. This was natural, the Chinese idea of community. Togetherness was a way of life.

But it wasn't all academic study for these kids. They had classes in art, in calligraphy, sports, drama, and music. At one school, there was an old Japanese World War II airplane on the playground. It was buffed and polished to a smooth finish, and children crawled all over it, pretending to be fighter pilots. Play was very much a part of each day too. I took a lot of pictures at the schools, thinking of my daughter and wondering how she was.

Our time in an art classroom was interesting. There were 50 kids to the classroom here too. Two kids to a table. They shared art supplies. We stood at the back and watched as a teacher at the front dipped her brush into watercolours and did a few strokes on a piece of paper taped to a board hanging on the wall. It was a landscape scene. Every child had an identical piece of paper taped to their board. They were making the very same marks, following right along with her. Step by step, they copied her every move. The result, of course, was 50 exact copies of the teacher's painting.

'That's a violation of copyright!' said Charon in a loud voice. She was fuming. 'They aren't copy machines! How are they supposed to learn anything about creativity?'

'But you have to admit, they *are* learning how to paint. It's pretty good.' Ed said, rubbing his cheek. 'They're learning a skill.'

Mr Ogawa stepped over to me and whispered, 'It's the same in Japan. They teach art this way, and then wonder why their art students aren't creative.'

'Maybe standing out is not highly valued in China or Japan,' I said.

'You're right. Even in Tokyo, which is the designated place for boldness, people conform to various *trends* in boldness, things that have already been done and are popular.'

'So, why are you here, Mr Ogawa, if you don't mind my asking? I'm curious.'

His eyes danced with intelligence.

'I found out American teachers were coming on this trip and I thought I might learn something from you Western devils.'

I couldn't help admiring Mr Ogawa's initiative.

Later that afternoon, we were ushered into the principal's office. He had his own interpreter. Dr Chin wore thick spectacles and was in excellent physical shape. His movements were quick and precise.

Once we were seated, he began speaking. We waited for the translation. He wanted to know about the arts curriculum at our schools. Guy whispered to us that he would not be contributing to the conversation, so as not to contaminate our answers. An interesting choice of words.

Charon raised her hand and was called on by Dr Chin.

'We don't have a central curriculum for art, or anything, really,' she said. 'There are local boards, made up of elected officials who decide what each school district will teach. And for art teachers, well, we pretty much decide on our own what art curriculum we will teach in our classroom. It gets approved by the school and then the board.'

The interpreter spoke Chinese to Dr Chin who listened, stared at Charon, frowned, and shook his head. He pointed to the door and it was clear the interpreter was being dismissed. We all looked stunned and turned to Guy. He just shook his head.

A moment later, a new man came through the door and asked to have the last statement repeated. Charon obliged. The same thing happened. Dr Chin stood up, glared at Guy and then bowed to us. He spoke again. The interpreter told us the interview was over. Dr Chin got up and left.

'Well. That's that,' Guy said. 'You see, the Chinese cannot believe that we don't have a single standardised curriculum of education in the United States. They just don't understand how on earth we could accomplish a goal if all the goals are different. I happen to agree with him. But there you go. Freedom and choice are essential to Americans, no matter what the cost. Not to the Chinese.' He stood up. 'I have a great place for us to go for dinner.'

We were met by Mrs Chen, a polite young woman, who was enthusiastic and quite attractive. She worked with Guy to arrange various activities for us. This was her government job and she was very proud of it. As we filed in to a dining room to eat, I asked Mrs Chen if she knew how I might get an email to my wife. She said she didn't. This was getting annoying.

We all sat around a large table where there was a huge Lazy Susan with many dishes to pass around. The smell was wonderful and I temporarily forgot my frustrations as I anticipated a good meal. There were about twenty varieties of mushrooms. Then they brought us steaming bowls of something that looked like a translucent spaghetti. We all took big helpings, especially Mrs Chen, who went after it with relish.

'Do you have children, Mrs Chen?' Ellen asked, as she slurped up the noodles. 'Mmmm. These are so good! I like the sauce too.'

'Yes. I have a baby boy.'

'Oh, how nice! Any pictures?'

Mrs Chen pulled out a dog-eared photo of a chubby baby smiling at the camera and her face softened with love and pride.

'My son.'

'Adorable! Who looks after him?'

'My parents. They live in Guilin. My husband and I were transferred here to Kunming.'

Ellen stared at her, eyes wide.

'You don't live with your child?'

Mrs Chen looked confused and then apologetic.

'I have permission to visit him twice a year.' She smiled at this as if it were a great privilege bestowed on her. Maybe it was, but I couldn't imagine only seeing Ariel twice a year.

'What is this delicious dish you've ordered for us, Mrs Chen?' Marie asked. 'Is it a kind of pasta?'

Mrs Chen bowed, grateful, no doubt, for the change of subject.

'This is cow's hooves,' she said. Big smile. 'They are sliced and boiled. A rare delicacy. Very good for the nails.' She held up her hands and showed off her beautiful red lacquered fingernails. Charon, who was sitting next to her, grabbed Mrs Chen's hand and inspected her nails.

'My God. They're real!'

# Chapter Seven

The next day we met Dr Sòng at the front of the hotel and boarded a bus. He was practically twitching with excitement. A delicate man, with a soft voice, Dr Sòng also had smooth hands with long tapered fingers. He was an expert in the 56 Nationalities in China, with a special interest in the Mosuo. Today, he had arranged for us to visit a Mosuo household.

Once we were seated, Guy took the microphone at the head of the bus, and after a few high-pitched whistles and squeaks, cleared his throat and started talking.

'Hello everyone! Just wanted to remind you today that there is absolutely no photography allowed on this field trip. There is an excellent book with photographs of the Mosuo people, which you can purchase at the end of the tour in the gift shop, though I'm sure Dr Sòng's book will be *much* better, when it comes out.'

Dr Sòng turned bright red and made a deep bow. He then handed him the microphone and Dr Sòng took it with those delicate hands of his.

'Good morning.' He coughed. It was a sound so soft I could barely hear it. 'Today we will visit a Mosuo family compound. There are around 50,000 of the Mosuo minority in China today. Most of them live here in the Yunnan and Sichuan provinces, and it is believed they migrated to the south a few centuries ago.

'They are a matriarchal culture and worship goddesses. The oldest female is the absolute ruler of the group. Everyone traces their lineage through their mother. The oldest woman holds the keys to the communal food stores.'

Charon flipped her hair and turned around in her seat to face me. I knew she was getting excited over this. It was another interesting aspect of Chinese culture involving women.

'The Mosuo have unique forms of marriage and family structure. When a young woman reaches marriageable age, she is given her own room so that she may choose a husband who will not live with her, but stay with his own family group and walk to the woman's home to stay with her at night. This is called a walking marriage.'

Charon raised her hand.

Dr Sòng called on her.

'How do they raise a child together?'

Dr Sòng swallowed and took his time answering.

'The child is raised by the mother's family, with the uncles playing a role. Not the father.'

'The father has no part in it whatsoever?' Charon asked.

'The father brings gifts to the family to help with financial support and he is free to visit as often as he wishes. But the males who help raise the child are the men living in the household, in the matriarchal home. The father doesn't live in

68

the home. He has his own duties to help raise children in his mother's house,' said Dr Sòng.

The bus pulled into the parking area while we all digested this information. I could not imagine not living with Katie and Ariel. I had a hard time understanding this system, yet, I could see the logic. Children were looked after, with lots of family around.

After leaving the bus, we followed Dr Sòng into a large fort-like structure, with Guy at the rear, no doubt keeping a watchful eye out for cameras. This building was made with large round timbers. A log cabin on a massive scale.

'This place looks formidable,' Ed said.

'Mosuo live in these structures for generations,' Dr Sòng said. 'They're built to last. The men do the heavy lifting and they work together. They are excellent builders. Both the men and women do the agricultural work for the benefit of the community, and it produces enough food for them to live on and some to sell. But the women do all the housework and manage the family. They assign all the jobs. These people are self-sufficient and no one starves.'

When we entered the building, we came to an open courtyard. There were cooking areas and places where food was being prepared. Men and women were working together, children too. They wore their unique tribal costumes. The women had big turban-style hats with beads strung around them. There were colourful outfits over white skirts and hand-woven scarves. The men wore straw hats with bright shirts and dark trousers.

'The Mosuo weave their own cloth,' Dr Sòng continued. 'Their clothing is distinctive. And there is individual variation to their costumes, another unusual thing that sets them apart from other Chinese Nationalities.'

Dr Sòng pointed to the loom in the far corner. A young woman pulled the bar close to her and then released it. She glanced over at us as she continued working.

Children raced around this busy complex. Old women with toothless grins and bent backs, walked around, touching shoulders affectionately, looking on at the work with pride.

Hetty raised her hand and Dr Sòng nodded in her direction.

'Do women ever divorce their walking husbands?'

Dr Sòng stood taller and cleared his throat.

'Oh yes. Many women and men dissolve their partnerships and start others. There is no stigma for divorce, or marriage. Women are not the property of men, nor are men the property of women. They stay together as long as they like. It doesn't matter. The family groups raise the children produced by these unions, because that is the value of the society. Children are protected and cherished and there is freedom to choose partners.'

'And there is no jealousy or fighting?' Charon asked.

'In the Mosuo language, there is no word for jealousy. No word for murder. No word for rape. These things are not part of their experience.'

We all stared at him.

The temptation to take pictures was excruciating. But not taking them gave me the chance to fully observe this unique group of people. They weren't just posing for tourists, though there was some of that, of course. They were genuinely proud of their unique culture. It was a baffling alternative to what we Westerners had assumed was normal.

Of course, in the end, there was a gift shop. Charon, Hetty and I bought the book about the Mosuo. Susie bought a scarf. Ed purchased an embroidered tablecloth for his wife. They used an abacus here too. I did not see a computer anywhere.

'Good thing you all bought something that doesn't weigh much,' Guy said, as we filed out of the compound toward the bus.

I turned to him, puzzled.

'Why's that?'

'Oh, Lord. I better tell everyone. It may have slipped my mind.'

Guy held up his hands and clapped. Everyone turned to face him.

'Sorry to interrupt. Glad you bought some things. It helps the community. And it's good to buy things that are lightweight. What you don't want to do is buy the stone bowls everyone seems to be crazy about. They weigh a ton.'

Ellen and Marie's eyebrows shot up.

'Why does that matter?' Marie said. 'We bought some yesterday.'

I wondered when they snuck out to buy stone bowls.

'We'll be flying to Beijing next week on Air China. They have weight limits. If you're loaded down with stoneware, it will be very expensive.'

'Now you tell us,' Ellen said.

# Chapter Eight

The next day was our day trip to Dali, a little town east of Kunming on the shore of Lake Erhai. It would take three hours to get there by bus. We had to go over a mountain, so it was important to get an early start. Guy was very excited about this trip. He said it was the first time he had been granted permission to see Yinshuo Island, where there was a very old village. No Westerners had ever been allowed before.

Once we were getting on the bus, he said, 'Did you all remember to bring little gifts? Shiny ones?'

'Oh no!' Charon cried. 'I left mine in my room. I'll be back in two shakes.'

Charon grabbed my sleeve and dragged me along with her as she ran toward the hotel.

'Why do I need to go?' I was stumbling along beside her.

'I wanted to remind you that the interview is in three days. In your room.'

'It's a crazy idea and I want no part of it.'

'Oh, you're already part of it. You can't back out now.'

'I never signed up for this. I'm not doing it, Charon.'

She stopped running, bent over with hands on knees to get her breath and composed herself. Then, the she-devil raised her spine, threw her shoulders back and I swear her eyes glowed red.

'If you don't do it, I will tell Guy you've taken pictures you shouldn't have taken and he will take your precious camera away. Forever. You'll never see those pictures again.'

How did she know I had good pictures on my camera? They were the best ones I'd ever taken.

'That's blackmail.'

'That's the deal.'

'You are insane. Your project is not worth these risks.'

'And your pictures. Are they worth the risking?'

She flicked her hair and started running again, a smile of victory on her lips.

I followed her. She had me by the balls.

We blasted through the front glass doors and took the stairs in leaps and bounds. When we got to her floor, we just about stumbled over the key girls who were all on their hands and knees, scrubbing the carpet with a toothbrush.

They all looked up at us, stunned. The girl who had Charon's key immediately stood up and ran to her door. Number 27. She fumbled with the enormous key ring, found the key and unlocked the door for us. Stepping back, she bowed her head.

Charon grabbed the little bag she had left on the table and hurried back out of the room. The girl closed and locked the door as we headed back down the stairs at a dead run.

'What was that all about?' I cried, as we ran toward the front door.

'Just shut up and get on the bus! I'll tell you later!'

The motor was running. We made a dash for it. I could see Katheryn and Susie hanging out of the window, slamming the side of the bus with the palm of their hands.

'Points! Points off for being late!'

Charon waved her middle finger at them as she ran beside the bus, which shut them up fast. I almost laughed, but thought better of it. We sank down in the front two seats as the wheels moved and we were off.

'Guy wouldn't really leave us,' I said.

'Oh, yes I would,' sang Guy a few seats behind us. 'But we need all the shiny objects we can get.'

As the voices were raised in excited chatter, I turned back to talk to Charon.

'Tell me about those key girls.'
She sighed.

'I suppose they're the lucky ones. They don't have to sell coal and live in a coal heap all their lives. Everyone here has a job and they're glad to have one, even if it means scrubbing a rug with a toothbrush.'

'But how boring and useless!'

'Yeah. It's awful, but what do we know? We're spoiled. At least they don't starve.'

The driver slammed on the brakes and we all went flying forward. Charon and I threw our hands out in an instinctive gesture to brace ourselves, when I caught the handrail and grabbed her around the waist with my other hand, just before she was about to crash through the windshield.

The driver laid on the horn, screaming at the car in front of him. We all drew in breath again and found our seats. Like the car I arrived in, there were no seat belts on the bus.

Guy mopped his forehead with his handkerchief. Even *he* was sweating.

'It's all right, everyone! Driving conditions here are...different than we're used to.'

'He's a maniac!' Katheryn yelled.

'It's not so easy!' Guy yelled back, surprising everyone. He sat up straight and composed himself before speaking again. 'A driving license in this country costs thousands of Yuan. And I assure you, it isn't easy to drive here with the road conditions. This isn't Beijing. The road structures aren't adequate here. It takes a lot of skill to get to Dali and our driver knows what he's doing. So, just hold on tight. Those of you who wish to offer prayers, feel free.'

'Are you saying this road isn't safe?' Susie asked.

Guy craned his neck around to face her.

'No adventure worth having is free of risk. We're going to Yinshuo Island. It's a privilege not granted to any other group. This is the only way to get there.'

Not a word was spoken after that. As we climbed up the mountain which separated us from our destination, the road grew steeper, rockier and closer to the precipice. By the time we neared the top, we all had our noses pressed against the windows and there were gasps, shrieks and whimpers as we kept nearing the cliff edge, a precipice that would lead to a certain death if we tumbled over it.

Guy just stared straight ahead – eyes boring through the windshield in silent support of our driver who seemed to be a road whisperer. He always knew where the edge of the cliff was and managed not to go over it.

'For the Love of GOD!' screamed Susie, suddenly losing it entirely. 'Let me off! Let me off this bus right now!'

Guy turned and spoke to her through clenched teeth. 'There is no place to let you off. BE QUIET. Our driver has to concentrate.'

I was a bit shocked at Guy's behaviour. Our captain was a being rather rude, but things were admittedly tense.

Susie's whimpering continued. It was the white noise of the remainder of our trip.

'If we die, Grant, I want you to know, I will never forgive you for abandoning me in my hour of need,' Charon said, in a casual voice.

'If we die now, Charon, how on earth will it matter?'

'I'd die knowing you weren't willing to help with my project.'

As she spoke, we felt a sudden juddering halt. A wheel had gone straight over the edge and the front of the bus dropped down a foot. We shrieked. The driver threw the gears into reverse, put his foot on the accelerator and gunned it. Miraculously, we backed up, found our groove, and continued down the road.

'OK,' I said. 'I'll help, if it makes you feel better.'

Charon squeezed my knee.

When we finally pulled into Dali there was smoke pouring out of the back of the bus. Our driver got out, slammed his door and lit up a huge cigar. He leaned back on the hood as he smoked, his arms crossed, not a care in the world.

Guy stood up and turned to us, white as a sheet, and trembling.

'Here we are. As promised.' His voice was shaky.

He took a moment to compose himself again. It was very disconcerting to see him like this. He had always been our rock of calm and confidence. Our leader.

Pulling a flask out of his pocket, he unscrewed the top. Slowly, he took a long drink and then screwed it back on and put it in his pocket as we watched, astonished.

'I hope you will all excuse me. That was my malaria medicine. I sometimes get flare ups. I hope you all remembered to take your malaria medicine today. It's very important.'

He looked around the bus expectantly and we all nodded.

'Good. Now. I have a little surprise for you. That long awaited 'free time' is here at last. You all have ninety minutes to explore the streets of Dali, grab some lunch, and meet back here for the next leg of our journey. It's going to be very exciting.'

'Where are you going to be?' Marie asked.

'I have a little errand. There are some details to work out for our donkey carts. You just run along and explore. Dali is tiny. You can't get lost.'

'You said Kunming was small, and it has two million people!' cried Katheryn.

Guy shot her a look that said *do not mess with me or you will regret it* and Katheryn said nothing further.

'Kunming is not as big as Beijing. Dali is not a big city like Kunming. Believe me. You'll be fine. The lake is a good landmark. And the three pagodas. You can't miss them.'

'But we don't know the language!' wailed Marie.

'Use sign language like everybody else! Act it out! Now get out of here! Beat it!'

He stomped down the aisle and off the bus. We saw him out the window. He was walking away from us in big strides.

We all sat very still for a few moments and then Mr Ogawa stood up and started moving down the aisle. Ed followed him. Then Ellen and Marie and the rest of us did the same, one by one.

Hetty and Charon took off together toward the town centre. The other ladies went behind them. When I stepped off the bus, I found Mr Ogawa and Ed waiting for me. Without a word, we strolled down the street in the opposite direction of the women.

'Gosh. I hope Guy's OK,' Ed said.

The three of us were quiet for a few moments.

'He just needs some 'me' time,' Mr Ogawa said in a soft voice. Then he laughed and Ed and I laughed too. Suddenly we were all right again. We walked down a deserted street in what looked like a residential neighbourhood. All the houses had those little grey tiled roofs which sat on them like hats. Built in the old style, with wood shutters, these homes looked as if they hadn't been painted in over a century.

Ed, being a resourceful guy, had managed to bring along a brochure about Dali. I wondered where he got such a thing, but wasn't surprised that he had one. He read as we walked. 'This is the oldest part of the old town, first formed in the tenth century, but later burned to the ground by Mongols. This Dali has been around since the fourteenth century, surviving takeovers, rebellions and even a massive earthquake in 1925.' It looked tired down to its bones. Everything was worn and faded.

'Maybe we should turn around or find a proper road. I'm getting hungry,' Ed said.

'I'm looking for a place to email my wife,' I said, though I seriously doubted we'd find one in Dali. The place looked much older than

Kunming. It didn't appear to need technology of this century.

'Look there,' Mr Ogawa said, lifting his chin.

We followed his gaze and saw a 1950s-style beauty parlour. A lady was sitting under a huge hairdryer reading a magazine. She wore Western style clothes, a long skirt and a white blouse.

'A noodle bar!' cried Ed, pointing further on. 'They should have something.'

We were delighted to find a place that was not too dissimilar from the breakfast place in Kunming and we ordered won ton soup and sesame balls with bean curd, like we were locals. Not that we spoke the language but we could point well.

After a very satisfying meal, Ed unfolded himself from his tiny chair and stood up. He stretched his hands above his head and then shook them out like he was about to run a race.

'I think we should split up,' Ed said. 'We can cover more ground that way. I want to see the pagodas.'

Mr Ogawa and I blinked at one another. This was a shocking thing to hear Ed say. We didn't expect this independent streak coming from him.

'That's a long walk from here,' Mr Ogawa said. 'Miles. You won't make it back in time.'

'I'm a fast walker, on my own.'

'Well, all right. I'd like to go to the lake. Do you want to come, Grant?'

This was my chance to take some pictures. Alone.

'No, thank you. I'll wander around here a bit more.'

Mr Ogawa sighed.

'Mr Anderson won't like us wandering around on our own. Didn't he say he preferred it if we went with someone when we had free time?'

'I won't tell,' Ed said.

Well. Ed was full of surprises.

'Deal.'

We all shook hands and parted with a wave.

'Back at the bus in forty-five minutes!' called Ed over his shoulder.

I waited until Ed and Mr Ogawa were no longer visible and then I picked a small street and wandered. Each house was fascinating. The faded paint colours on the wood shutters, the

86

grass growing on the older roofs, clothes on a line, signs of life. I took out my Nikon D-70 and started snapping – the familiar sound was comforting. Little gears. Shutters. Motors. Drives. The sound of photographs being made.

I knew just what I'd do when I edited them on my computer. I wanted to capture that fadedness, to sort of bleach the colours. This was what I was after. A chance to take pictures. To play with the idea of time. This peaceful village, centuries old and barely disturbed, was what I wanted to explore, all by myself.

As I walked, I came across a local, a man bent over with a bulging sack on his back. He looked up, surprised to see me. I smiled, holding my camera and he smiled back, his face unguarded. He was used to tourists. He spoke to me. I shrugged.

'I'm sorry. I don't understand.'

'Ni Hao!' he said.

'Ni Hao!' I knew that one!

He laughed from his belly and continued on his way. I must have seemed a strange sight to him, but not unheard of.

I wondered what villagers on Yinshuo would think of us. Why was Guy bringing us here? Surely not to show us progressive methods of teaching art. He was certainly going to great lengths to show us this place. Who was he trying to impress? Us? Or his Chinese bosses?

This made me think of his outburst on the bus, of his 'medicine' and I had a sudden feeling of sympathy for him. Here was a Midwesterner, far from home, living in a strange land. I wondered if he had family back in Wisconsin, or if he felt lonely here. He never talked about himself, but stuck to the program. His Chinese seemed perfect to me. It must have taken him a long time to learn.

Another tiny street appeared and I turned and walked down it. Even quieter than the other one. I heard my own footsteps crunch the gravel on the road, tiny stones under my feet. The houses were even closer together, smaller. Roofs were sagging, the paint gone from all but the grooves of the shutters. Everything sun-bleached. Old. Most of the windows were closed against the heat of the day.

Then, I heard a noise. A faint one. The sound floated above my head, and I turned all around trying to catch it. What was it? A violin? A pipe? It grew louder as I drew nearer.

Finally, I stood before an open window. As I peered into the depths of what I thought was a house, I realised my mistake. It was a barber shop. There were jars of combs and old-fashioned razors laid out on the counter. No one was in the shop, but the sound continued to float out to the street.

A shaft of light pierced the darkness and as my eyes adjusted, I could see three men in the back, bent over together. One played a pipe, another, a Chinese accordion, and the third, some sort of strange instrument I'd never seen before. The sound coming from it was wistful but melodic, with low notes, deep and resonant, and high notes like the sighs of a woman.

My hands pulled the camera to my eye and my fingers found the stops and twisted the dial until I could feel the clicks hit the grooves. I set up my shot and pressed the button. It was just after this that one man noticed me, and then the others turned their heads in my direction.

I lowered my camera and waved.

They stared at each other and then back at me. One man stood up and made his way to the front of the shop, to the open window closer to where I stood.

'Can I help you?' he said, in perfect English.

I was so surprised to hear those words, it took me a few moments to respond.

'I'm sorry. I didn't mean to disturb you. The music was so beautiful.'

He bowed and raised his arm. He was holding the strange instrument by the neck with one hand. His face broke into a smile in the golden afternoon light. His eyes were kind. There were wrinkles in the corners.

'Please. Won't you join us?' he asked. I was taken aback. He motioned me forward with a beckoning hand as he came around and opened the door to his little shop. I followed him back to the other two men who bowed.

'These are my friends. Liu and Ti. I'm Zhao.'

'I'm Grant Decker. How nice to meet you.' Out of habit, I stuck out my hand and Mr Zhao grabbed it and pumped it hard as he giggled.

'I haven't done that in such a long time,' he said, wistfully.

'Your English is excellent.'

He nodded and bowed. Polite in both languages.

'I went to university in America. NYU! Twenty-one years ago.'

'Wow! What were you studying?'

'Music! But I never finished my degree.'

'Oh?'

'I had to come back. 1989. Tiananmen Square. I was afraid for my parents. Some students were told not to come back. They were afraid of trouble here. But I didn't want to leave them here. My father was the town barber. This was his shop. He left it to me when he died in 1990. I've been the town barber ever since.'

'Town barber. That's quite a legacy.'

'It is.'

'Do you miss American music?'

'Oh yes. I liked it very much. Jazz. I remember it well. But we do what we can with our little band here. We practice our music. Every day, at lunch time.'

He held up the instrument he was playing with the two strings.

'What *is* that?'

He laughed like a child.

'ErHu! It's like a violin, only with two strings. Not four.'

'The sound is beautiful. Will you play some more?"

He needed no further coaxing and sat on the edge of his low stool, pulling the delicate instrument on his lap and dragging the bow across the strings. He nodded to his friends, who adjusted their positions and joined in.

Once more the street was filled with the melody of music and I saw these men playing together in rapture, their eyes closed, fingers flying, ears twitching as they followed along. Three songs later, I glanced down and saw the time on my watch.

'I'm so sorry, but I have to catch a bus! Thank you for the concert.'

I turned to go, but Mr Zhao called me back.

'Take this with you,' he said, handing over the ErHu.

'What? I can't take your ErHu.'

'Please. It's a gift. I have another. Your gift has been allowing me the pleasure of speaking your language again and in so doing, bringing back my memories of America. Please accept this gift with my gratitude.'

When he put it that way, how could I refuse? I bowed deeply and said, 'XieXie,' which I hoped meant thank you. Then I bolted down the street, carrying my new instrument in one hand and my camera bag in the other.

When I arrived, everyone else was on the bus.

'Points!' yelled Marie.

'Sorry! Lost track of time.'

I slipped into a seat near Guy.

'Good God. An ErHu. Who sold you that?'

'No one. It was a gift.'

'Well, just do us all a favour and do not attempt to play that thing!'

'It's a Chinese violin. It's beautiful.'

'Not in the hands of a Westerner, I assure you. It can make horrible noises too if you don't know what you're doing.'

I kept quiet and instead enjoyed my secret joy at getting a chance to take photographs that were mine alone.

As we drove to our pick-up point for the donkey carts, I wondered why the scene of the musicians in the barber shop had been so striking. I realised it was familiar. I had seen it before. A Norman Rockwell painting called 'Shuffleton's Barbershop.' That was it! The darkened, empty front of a barbershop in the foreground, a light coming from a back room where the three men played a violin, a cello and a clarinet. It had the same intensity, concentration and rapture, the same love of the music.

Once we arrived, Guy hurried us off the bus and onto our next ride. Four to a cart. When the driver snapped a light whip at their flank, the donkeys took off down the road and we bumped along surprisingly fast toward a makeshift dock in the distance. There was the sound of tiny bells, almost like sleighbells as the donkeys trotted along, and I felt the wind in my hair.

When we came to a stop there were four muscled men waiting for us and two well-used fishing boats. After dividing ourselves between the boats, we were soon moving on the water toward our destination, Yinshuo Island.

The wind was strong and carried us fast, the waves lapping at our sides, refreshing us with the occasional splash. It only took twenty minutes and soon our fishermen were in the water, hauling us and the boat to the shoreline. It was a tricky operation for Susie and Katheryn, who were having trouble getting out, until the fishermen grew tired of waiting and just picked them up and put them down in the shallow water. They were a bit flustered at getting their feet wet, but moved to joined the rest of us.

'Gather round, everyone! And welcome to Yinshuo!' Our Guy was back.

# Chapter Nine

Guy shielded his eyes from the bright sunlight as he gleefully delivered his instructions to us. We stood there in a huddle watching his face.

'The Bai people live on these two islands. The larger population is over on Jinsuo, just north of us. It's had tourism for years now. There's even a hotel. The villagers there do performances of their customary dances. And they even have an underground dragon temple.

But the village here, on Yinshuo, has never been seen by Westerners. We're the first!'

'Do they have a school?' Katheryn asked, fanning herself with a recently bought dragon fan.

'Indeed, they do! And we're going to see it.'

'How did you arrange this?' Ellen was the suspicious type. But come to think of it, how did he?

'Strange as it may seem, they have the Internet here! With one computer. It's at the top of the hill, in the school. I've been emailing Mr Lin. And here he comes now!'

Walking toward us was an unsmiling little man, another fisherman from the look of his clothes. His shirt was grey and had holes in it. He wore a straw hat and thin leather sandals that took the shape of his feet. When he saw Guy, his eyes grew large and he came over and bowed repeatedly.

Guy spoke in a halting, awkward way. When Mr Lin seemed puzzled, I realised it must have been a dialect Guy wasn't too familiar with. Eventually, Mr Lin indicated that he understood and asked us to follow him.

'Now stay very close. No wandering about on your own. First stop is the temple, to pay our respects to the village Gods.'

He didn't have to convince us to stay close. The place was so quiet it was eerie. It was like walking into a ghost town. You could hear our steps on the gravelly road as we trudged up the steep slope of the hill toward the buildings of the village. The houses we could see were crumbling with age.

'Where is everybody?' Charon said to me in a whisper as she walked.

'Shhhh.'

I thought I saw a child dart between buildings, like a spectre.

We trudged on. Loudly. Seagulls scattered in the air before us, calling out in their mournful cry. A red cloth fluttered ahead of us, covering a doorway.

Mr Lin stepped up and parted the curtain, going inside. One by one we entered the dark space, the room thick with the scent of jasmine and musk. As our eyes adjusted, a row of statues appeared on an altar table, about 12 inches high. They were brightly painted Gods in human form, each wearing rich robes. They didn't seem threatening, exactly, but commanded respect. Their eyes were burning bright. Strands of flowers, beads and shells draped their necks.

'Please join me in paying respect to the God Benzhu, the God of prosperity and good fishing. These are his attendants,' Guy said.

Guy had done his homework. He had his hands together in a praying position, just like Mr Lin. His eyes were closed, and he was humming a low tone. We did the same. Not everyone was humming, but *I* gave it a good try. The humming and chanting went on for about five minutes, and then Mr Lin lifted his head, turned around, and went out the front door. Prayers done, we followed him.

Back in the bright sunlight, our host pointed to the hill, and we could see the radio and Internet towers there, as well as a modern building.

'Guy? Where are all the people of the village?' Ellen asked.

'Patience. They're just staying out of the sun. Have your objects ready.'

As if on cue, an old man ventured out of the shadows of one door. He sported a long white beard and shaggy eyebrows under a straw hat. He studied us carefully. Here was someone living in another century, right before our very eyes.

Ed stepped up to him and held out a small plastic magnifying glass – the type you might get as a child's prize in a cereal box. The old man studied Ed before letting his eyes rest on the object.

He turned his old head this way and that, frowned, then crossed his arms.

Ed demonstrated, moving the glass over his own hand.

The old man drew closer, observing the magnifying glass that make Ed's fingernail grow huge. He frowned, not understanding, then stepped back and folded his arms again.

He called out something in his language – words, like a spell. Perhaps he was calling us evil foreigners. After a moment, a few heads popped out of the dark windows to see us. Children mostly. Then adults. The old man drew closer to Ed and held out his hand. Ed placed the magnifying glass in it and bowed. Then he stepped back slowly like he was in a mine field.

'I think he likes it,' Ed said in a low voice.

The old man put his finger to the lens and touched it. Plastic. He had probably never touched plastic before, and I wondered what he thought of it. He let out a yip of shock as he saw it magnify his own fingernail. Then he laughed and tried the trick again. There was laughter coming from inside the house behind him.

More people came out, staring at us, but soon their attention turned to the gift. It was passed around and people played with it, trying to magnify other parts of their faces and hands. Someone brought out a fish and magnified its eyes. This brought smiles and laughs. One man patted Ed on the back. He clearly approved of the gift.

'Let's move on,' Guy said. 'Mr Lin wants us to see the classroom. It's only recently been built. Brand new.'

We followed Mr Lin up the hill. I wasn't sure how old he was. He had no grey hairs or saggy skin. He was tough and his tight muscles must have come from the hard work of fishing. He was chatting to Guy, who nodded and appeared to understand.

'They mostly eat fish here,' he called to us. 'They also trade with farmers in Dali. They have cornmeal, rice and flour. His wife is cooking something for us today. We're invited to tea.'

'Is it—'

Guy turned around and Susie changed her mind about her question.

As we went along the road, more people peeked out at us and we heard the giggling of children. Charon held out a marble in her outstretched hand to a little girl who stared at it as if it were a star. Other children came around. All of them were dressed in very worn and faded clothes. It was hard to imagine how they managed in this place. The buildings had large holes in the roofs. We saw very little furniture or any sign of comfort, but we could smell cooking.

When we left the village buildings, the road got steeper. I began to wonder if children would come all this way to a school. It was getting hotter and more difficult to climb, but finally we made it.

The radio and Internet tower were impressive, especially for a village with no plumbing or heating. We stepped inside the cool of a modest building and once our eyes adjusted to the dim light, I noticed a school table with a couple of chairs and a blackboard on the wall with two horsehair erasers, standard issue in a Chinese classroom. There were a few books on a bookshelf, but no sign that any of these things were in use.

We waited for Guy to fill us in. He said nothing, as if waiting for further information himself.

In the far corner of the little room was another small table with a radio transmitter and receiver, headphones and a table microphone. Next to this was a wood box with a lock. Mr Lin approached the table, took out a key from his pocket and unlocked the box. Inside was a Chinese laptop. He didn't bother to power it up but pointed to it and at Guy, then spoke fast. Guy listened and pondered the meaning of what he said.

'Ah.' He glanced back at Mr Lin. 'This is where he communicates with the Chinese government and where he read my email request to visit.'

Guy tried out some more words on the man and eventually, after some shrugging, hand gestures and a bit of laughter, something was communicated.

'Mr Lin said the school hasn't happened yet. The villagers don't see the need. They are content with the way things are. He hopes to someday hire a teacher. It's early stages at the moment. They have the curriculum from the government, but can't read it very well as it isn't in their language.'

'Can we go back now?' Susie asked. 'I'd like to see more of Dali.'

Guy ignored her.

'We're going back down the hill to Mr Lin's home now, where his wife has prepared tea and cakes for us.'

He pulled his shoulders back, lifted his head and followed Mr Lin out the door. We filed out and descended the hill, single file, like donkeys, and did not say a word. We had no idea of what awaited us.

The view from the top of the island was of the village below and the sea beyond. There was a cluster of about twenty very old houses, most with caved-in roofs. What kind of hospitality could these people offer? The best of their offerings must go to the temple to honour their Gods. We were mere Westerners. Yet, hospitality was being offered.

The hike down the hill left us hot and thirsty. We arrived at the place where Mr Lin and his family lived. It was much like all the others, only with a very old door. It was perhaps one of the few doors that remained intact after the big earthquake.

Mr Lin banged on it with his fist and it opened immediately. A woman, presumably his wife, bowed her head in greeting. If she was terrified by the sight of us, she didn't show it. She stepped aside to let us into her home, one with damaged roof and a dirt floor.

Mr Lin spoke, extending his hand. He was introducing his wife, who nodded to us as she held her hands together. She was dressed in an outfit similar to the Mosuo. She wore a large headdress with strings of beads and a black skirt with an apron covered in embroidered designs. Behind her were two children, a young boy and an older girl. There was a fire pit and I could smell the corn cakes cooking on a heated stone. A teapot was next to it. We were invited to sit on cushions. All ten of us took our seats on the floor.

'Say, Guy? How come these villagers get two children?' Ed asked.

'Minority populations get two. The Bai are a minority. Like the Mosuo.'

Mrs Lin put some large leaves inside the teapot and placed it over the fire. Very soon, there was a strong smell of the burning leaves. Then she took a wooden spoon and broke up the heated leaves, poured water into the pot and set it back on the fire.

As the tea steeped, she took a wood spatula and removed the corn cakes onto an earthenware plate and Mr Lin passed them around. They were still warm and sweet. Corn cakes with squash in them. I'd never tasted anything like it. They were excellent.

When the tea was ready, it was poured into teacups and we each took one. We were all on our best behaviour. Even Susie didn't ask any questions. And from her face, I could see she didn't object to the tea. It was surprisingly refreshing. Full of flavour.

We all bowed to our hosts and listened to them talk with Guy in a Chinese dialect he could hardly decipher. Now that the formalities of having tea with Mr Lin and his family were nearly done, I waited anxiously to depart.

'This would be a good time to give parting gifts,' Guy said. He took out a gift from his pocket. 'A compass!' He unfolded the old army compass and showed it to Mr Lin who watched the dial and observed how it moved when Guy turned around in a circle. He was intrigued. The smile on his face was huge and he bowed to Guy, words of gratitude pouring from his lips.

Charon then stood up from her cushion and went to Mrs Lin, holding up a blue cat's eye marble. She held it to the light of the window and it sparkled like a diamond. There were gasps of delight from the entire family who stared back at Charon as if *she* might be a Goddess. To cement this notion, Charon presented each child with a marble too. A green and a gold. There were more bows, more words in the unknown tongue.

Charon had really scored points here. No one else offered anything. Nothing, it seemed, could top this.

'You know, these gifts will probably go straight to the temple. They use anything shiny as an offering to their gods,' Guy said, rather smugly.

Charon waited a beat, then flipped her hair.

'Then, I suppose, the compass will go there too.'

Guy grimaced. He hadn't thought of that.

'I have a gift,' I blurted out, feeling like the third Wise Man. Digging in my rucksack, I carefully avoided the ErHu and pulled out my little polaroid camera. Everyone was staring at me. 'Come outside. My gift needs the light.'

Guy frowned.

'I don't think this is such a good idea.'

'A family portrait? They'll love it!'

I moved to the door and opened it. Everyone followed me outside and I arranged the little family in the sunlight. The other villagers had been hanging around and now moved in close to see what I was going to do. They watched as I posed the family, motioned for them to stay still, and smile. I stood back a few feet.

Raising the viewfinder to my eyes, I saw them in the crosshairs and snapped the picture. The polaroid groaned as it spit out the black square and all the eyes of the villagers grew big. I motioned for them to come closer and watch. They approached with caution, heads lowered to see the black square which began to change.

Everyone held their breath.

When the chemicals did their magic and the faces of the Lin family came into view – everyone screamed and ran in a different direction. Only the ten of us were left standing there.

'Nice going, toots.' Charon flipped her hair.

# Chapter Ten

That night I dreamed that Charon stood at the river Styx demanding a coin to ferry me across to the land of the dead. I woke up in a cold sweat. At that moment, there was the unmistakable sound of a mosquito buzzing around my head and I strained to recall if I had taken my malaria medicine that day. Sitting up in bed, I put my hands together and prayed to *my* Goddesses, Katie and Ariel. I missed them terribly and wanted only to be home with them. But there were no ruby slippers handy. I opened my eyes and I was still in China.

Guy had lectured us about every possible disease we could get, and there were many, but he had warned that the worst one was homesickness. He said it in such a way that we knew he was an expert. In an uncharacteristic moment of bare honesty, Guy told us that there was a high turnover rate of Americans who came to the university to teach. He had recruited them himself. But they didn't last six months. It was just too different for them. It seemed Guy was doomed to stay because he had become so good at the language that he'd proved himself to be indispensable. He had also, he said, come to love the Chinese people.

Well, I could see a lot to like about them. China was much more complex and interesting than I had imagined, but I loved my family and I needed them. Now. It was especially distressing to think that I was still part of Charon's plan and that she could very easily get us both landed in a Chinese jail if anyone found out about her little documentary project.

After our visit to Yinshuo Island, Guy told me if he ever saw me take the polaroid camera out again, he would take both my cameras away. He was quite serious about this. I had no credit left with him. I was skating on thin ice and I'll admit it, I was scared.

I listened to the buzzing mosquito while I waited for the dawn, and when it finally came, I leapt out of bed, grabbed the thermos of boiled water from outside the door, and brushed my teeth while hatching a plan.

Today we were going to visit Xishan Mountain, climbing to the top where there was a former monastery. Apparently, there was a fantastic view of Kunming from there, one well worth the climb. Guy said there were some small shops up there too, where we could buy souvenirs. I reckoned if there was an Internet tower on a little island like Yinshuo, this place on the mountain might have one too. Maybe there would be some way to email Katie. I had to try.

Our bus arrived in a cool mist around the base of the mountain. Already there was a line of Chinese tourists waiting at the gate. Guy held our tickets up in his hand, spread out like a fan.

'I'm not going with you to the top,' he announced. 'I have a heart condition.' It was stunning to realise Guy was not as vigorous and healthy as he at first seemed to be.

Susie and Katheryn put their heads together and had a private conference.

'You can go at your own pace. I've asked Mr Ogawa to hang back and bring up the rear, to be sure everyone is safe and accounted for. I've given him a walkie-talkie so he can be in touch with me.'

As we got off the bus, the mood was as sombre as the mist.

'Hey, now. It's going to be very enjoyable. Just you wait. There's even a costume hut on the way up, where you can dress up like Attila the Hun or an Empress and take pictures of one another.'

'We can take pictures then?' I asked.

'Yes. *This* is most definitely a tourist site. Take all the pictures you want, for your own personal use. But keep it pictures of yourselves and the view.'

'The costumes sound fun,' Ellen said. 'Let's go.' She went off, arm in arm with Marie.

Hetty grabbed Charon and they went off together too, and I went along with Ed. Mr Ogawa trailed behind Susie and Katheryn, who I suspected would find a bench and sit the hike out.

The trail hugged the side of the mountain and was, at first, quite wide and well worn. It started getting steep and hard to climb about half-way up. There were many rest benches and I noticed Ed taking advantage of them. He got out of breath several times.

'Are you all right?'

'Oh, I'm fine. Really. Why don't you go on ahead? We're doing this at our own pace, remember?' I couldn't see his face in the shade from his hat.

'Right. Well, if you're sure.'

'Go on. I'll be fine. I'll probably walk with Mr Ogawa.'

I nodded and waved. This would help with my plan, which was to sprint ahead of Charon and the others and find a way to email up there without anyone knowing.

Picking up my pace, I passed Ellen and Marie who were in Chinese silk dresses at the costume hut, taking pictures of themselves.

'Oh, Grant! Would you take a picture of us?'

I obliged and they were thrilled. Then I hurried on.

At one of the observation points there was a crowd of Chinese tourists taking in the view of Kunming. The mist cleared and it was stunningly beautiful in the sunlight. You could see everything from up here – almost an aerial view.

As I took it in, I noticed a family nearby. The man was taking a picture of a woman and her son, who looked about eight or nine. The woman stood out because she was a highly decorated military officer.

'Well, look at her!' Charon said.

I jumped.

'Don't sneak up on me like that!'

She laughed.

'I wasn't sneaking. Do I make you nervous, Grant?'

'No. Of course not.'

'Day after tomorrow is the big day. Sunday. Two o'clock. In your room.'

'How do you know we'll have free time then?'

'It's on the schedule! Keep up, toots.'

I frowned.

'No one gave me a new schedule.'

'We leave for Beijing on Monday. Early. Guy gave us Sunday afternoon and evening to pack. No scheduled events. Don't forget your ErHu.' She smirked. Then she pinched my ass! I turned my head around, but in the crowd, no one had seen.

'I'm walking on,' I said. She smiled at me in that way of hers, like she was going to have her way, no matter what.

After moving on, I turned back to see Charon waving at me. Hetty was busy taking pictures of the view. I had to hurry now if I was going to get any time on the top of this mountain alone.

It was almost noon when I got to the top, tired, out of breath, and very sweaty. Conveniently, there was a woman selling bottled water for two Yuan. I paid and drank up. Relief at last.

Walking on, I came to what was left of the walls of an old monastery which was now a carnival of free enterprise. There must have been 50 people hawking their wares for tourists, yelling at full volume in a place that must once have been a haven of peace and tranquillity.

I surveyed the scene, looking for any kind of computer, anywhere. There were cheap costumes, plastic swords, Attila the Hun hats and stone bowls.

Then I saw a table covered with Chairman Mao merchandise. The face, made familiar by Andy Warhol, was everywhere. I picked up a lighter with his image on it and opened it. A little tune played, sounding tinny and far away.

A toothless old woman stood up behind the table and started singing along energetically, swinging her arms. She'd probably sung this song during the revolution.

'How much?' I asked.

'20 Yuan.'

I thought over the presents for my family. The book on the Mosuo tribe was for Katie. The ErHu for Ariel. I didn't really need another present. I put it back on the table. The old lady grabbed my arm.

'You smart. I have something much better for you.' She shook her finger at me, grinning. Without her eyes leaving mine, she put another lighter in my hand. Looking down I saw a younger Mao, with a yellow background and a slimmer face. There was a glow around him, a distinct halo effect.

'What's this?'

'Young Mao! Like when I first see him! Rare. You like?'

I was sceptical, but I did like. There was something both innocent and terrible about this face.

'How much?'

'Collector item. Rare.'

'How much?'

'200.'

'What? 200 Yuan?' I put it down like it had burned my hand and turned to go.

'Wait!'

I sighed and turned back. I really wanted that lighter, for reasons I couldn't quite define, even to myself. Maybe I could haggle. Guy told us it was the fun part for these merchants. If I didn't bargain, they would be insulted.

She frowned at me.

'180. For you.'

I tightened my fists. The game was on.

'150.'

'Done!'

*What? That was it?*

She held out her hand. I blinked, then took out my money. It was around 20 US dollars. She plucked it away and handed me the lighter. I obviously didn't understand the principle of haggling, but never mind. It was mine now. And I was happy with my young Mao lighter. I slipped it into my pocket. At least it was lightweight. It wasn't a stone bowl.

I walked on and refocused on my goal and then I saw it. A sign. In English. Sort of.

I N T R N E T   C A F e

I ran to the little tent where a man was at a table with a keyboard and an old blue Bondi Mac. Wow. An antique. But it must still be working.

Sitting down at the keyboard, I was flooded with hope, like the young Mao in my pocket.

'Email?' I was used to speaking in broken English now, like the Chinese merchants.

'20 Yuan, 20 minutes,' he said, flatly. I sensed no bargaining here. No spirit of fun about it. I preferred it this way.

After handing him the 20 Yuan, he typed on the keyboard and made Google appear before me. In English. I nearly started crying in relief. This was my connection to home – to Katie, to Ariel. Once I was into my account, I saw the 37 emails from Katie.

They started out playful.

'Having fun?' I could hear her voice in my head.

'You must be really busy.'

'When are you going to call?'

Then, they got worried.

'Haven't heard from you.'

'Everything all right?'

'You must not have Internet access. I thought you might not.'

Then, they got angry.

'You couldn't find a computer?'

'They have land lines in China.'

'What am I supposed to think?'

It crushed me, causing her to worry like this. But it wasn't my fault. Was it? I should have looked harder for a way to email her. I should have put my foot down with Guy about using a phone. I looked at my watch. I had to hurry. Time was almost up and the rest of them would be along any minute now.

But what could I say in my email to Katie? I KNEW the Chinese government would probably be reading emails. They were censoring the Internet! I suddenly remembered how Charon said we could be locked up if the Chinese thought we were spies. I couldn't tell Katie about Charon's project or that she might report me to Guy for taking pictures that would get me in trouble. I couldn't say a damn thing!

I looked at Katie's last email to me. Yesterday.

'I'm not gonna lie. I don't think Cassandra misses you, but she's been acting strange lately. Complaining more than usual. Like something's not right.'

*Cassandra is correct!* I silently screamed. And then I started my email to Katie and the Chinese government.

'Dear, darling, wife,

Just wanted you to know I'm fine.

Love,

Your husband'

It was a lie and Katie would know it. I've never sent such a short email in my life. It would worry her more than no email.

I tried again.

'Oh darling,

Oh, how I miss you! Oh. Oh. Oh. How I miss you! You have NO idea. Guy won't let me use the phone here. Remember the movie with Dr No? Well, Guy is like that. And it hasn't been easy to find a computer with the Internet here either.

I wish I could come home right now, before anything bad happens, like it could on our last day here before we go to Beijing. See the schedule from Charon on my computer. You know the password. I'd really, really like to hear your voice, just once before we leave the hotel. You have the name of the university on a piece of paper on your desk. Did you know they own the hotel where we are staying? Well, they do. Love, your husband.'

'Time up! You want more 20 minutes?'

'There you are!' It was Charon and Hetty. Coming into the tent.

I hit send and closed the window, then fell out of my chair trying to get up, just as they were coming over to me.

'Hi, Grant,' Hetty said, crossing her arms as I dusted myself off. 'What are you up to?'

'Nothing. Just checking email.'

'We gotta go,' Charon said. 'Now. Ed's had a panic attack.' She turned and walked to the tent door with Hetty, then looked back at me. 'Come on, Grant! Chop Chop!'

# Chapter Eleven

As it turned out, Ed recovered quite quickly. He was apologising, all the way down the mountain. He'd never been scared of heights before. Maybe it was the food the other day. The sun. Everyone was sympathetic and I'm sure Susie and Katheryn were quite happy to be going back early.

Marie and Ellen were still wearing the costumes I'd photographed them in. They had bought them to take home and wear in their third-grade classrooms. Wouldn't the children love it? I pulled out my Mao lighter to show the gang.

'Oh, I've got one of those,' Katheryn said.

I was stunned.

'It's a fake, actually,' Guy said.

I was double-stunned.

'A fake what?'

'The Old Mao is the real one. They were becoming scarce, so some enterprising rascal commissioned found an old picture, photoshopped it and put it on a low-cost lighter. How much did you pay for that?'

I put my lighter away. I still liked it.

When we rolled into the hotel and got out, Guy told us we had free time until our lunch tomorrow with Dr Sòng. He had invited all of us to his home.

'Now, please dress up for the visit and prepare to be honoured. This is very personal. Dr Sòng must like you. He's never done this before.'

A murmur of approval went around. Dr Sòng was a likeable man.

'Where does he live?' Marie asked.

'Like many people in the south of China, he lives on the site of his job. Like the key girls, it's his job for life.'

'For life?' Marie was trying to imagine being a key girl for life. We all were. To Americans the idea of having no choice in your job was, well, unimaginable.

'That's right. It's job security like none of us will ever experience in America. The government gives you a job, an income for your working life, which ends at age 55. You also get free healthcare for your entire life and you get a home for life too. You don't have much to worry about. Since Mao's time, the average lifespan has been extended from age 40 to 75.'

'But what about freedom? What about individuality?' Hetty cried. 'What about human rights?'

Guy shrugged. 'What about community? Security? Freedom from want? Freedom from crime? What about more years of being free from a job? Most of us drop dead before we even retire in the US.'

It got quiet then. We could see his point.

'Anyway, to answer your question, Marie, Dr Sòng lives in one of the classrooms at the university. With his wife and daughter.'

'A classroom? But where do they cook?'

'They share a communal kitchen in one of the buildings and—' Guy straightened his tie. 'There's a communal lavatory on each floor.'

The next day found us sitting in Dr Sòng's classroom-home. We sat on wooden chairs in a circle. The room was about 20 feet by 30 feet. There was a curtain blocking one side of the room, behind which was a bed that could just fit two people and a bedroll that was for the couple's child.

Dr Sòng was even more softspoken and polite in his own home, giving us a shy smile as he introduced his wife and child. He carried a large pot into the room, set it down on a chair and lifted the lid. This one pot meal was made by his wife in the communal kitchen. I could smell mushrooms, carrots, potatoes, peas, curry and spices. He dished a generous amount into a bowl which his daughter, about six years old, brought to each of us, along with a pair of chopsticks. I was praying that Susie didn't ask if it was safe to eat.

As we tucked into the food, Ed leaned over and spoke to Guy in a low voice, so Dr Sòng would not hear.

'About how much money does Dr Sòng make in a year?'

I heard and stared at him.

'I'm just curious!' Ed said, defensively.

Guy swallowed his bite of the stew and wiped his mouth with a paper napkin.

'Dr Sòng makes the equivalent of about 600 US dollars a year.'

Ed blinked.

'Shocking, isn't it?' Guy went on. 'Kind of puts things in perspective.'

'At least he has job security,' Ed said.

'He does.'

'Have you ever thought of inviting him to America?' I asked, in a low voice.

'Dr Sòng would love to come to America. I looked into it for him, once. And the government would like to have him promote his book in

America. But he declined. He has a family here. He doesn't want to leave them.'

I understood that, feeling pangs of guilt for leaving mine. You can feel very lost in a wildly different place like America. Even Americans felt that way.

My eyes roamed across the classroom for clues about Dr Sòng. He didn't teach in this room. It was his personal space, if you had such a thing in China. The blackboards were blank, the erasers resting on the ledge with some chalk. Perhaps his daughter drew on the boards sometimes. A large map of China adorned one wall, marked with his research on the 56 Nationalities. There were stacks of files on his desk, notebooks and pens. Books were piled in the corners and along the walls behind our chairs. There was one picture on the wall, of his daughter, Mae, smiling shyly. Mae was his treasure. His one photograph.

When we finished eating, Mrs Sòng took our bowls and bowed graciously as we complimented her cooking. I had no idea if she understood English, but every move she made was warm and welcoming.

Dr Sòng stepped into the centre of the room and announced that Mae wished to do a dance for us. Then he stood back and pressed the button of an old tape recorder as little Mae took her place, eyes forward staring out into an imaginary audience behind us.

The music was being played on an ErHu and once again the hauntingly beautiful melody danced in the air, reminding me of the barbershop in Dali.

Mae was wearing a simple leotard with a pink gauze skirt and slippers. Her wrists were bent, her fingers splayed in a highly stylized way. She moved with a grace beyond her years and we realised she had been practicing for a long time. This was an offering that touched me. One made by a six-year-old child, by Mrs Sòng, by Dr Sòng, because he humbly offered to share his life and his home with us.

We clapped with enthusiasm when it was over. Dr Sòng bowed to us and smiled, so proud of his little girl. His one child. He then served lychees to us for dessert. We ate slowly.

Guy was sitting next to me and I asked him the question burning in my mind, in a low voice.

'Do they have cold winters here?'

'Yes. Snow sometimes.'

I thought of how cold the UK was to me, coming from California. I had to learn so many new habits, trying to stay warm. Hot tea several times a day. Layers and layers of clothes, boots, wellies, jumpers, anoraks, coats and scarves. Our closets were stuffed with all this gear for the three of us. For snow, we had even more things like gloves and snow shovels.

'Where does he keep all his cold weather stuff?'

Guy rubbed his face. A bad sign. He glanced at me like I was an idiot and then looked away.

'You see the suit he is wearing?'

I nodded.

'He has another one just like it. He has only two. And he wears both of them in the winter.'

Of course. A man earning 600 dollars a year couldn't afford winter stuff. He did without it. It dawned on me in that moment that as an American, I had been programmed to buy things from the moment I was born. We all had to work out how to get money to *buy* things, but we learned to think this was essential to our happiness. Only the more stuff we got, the more money we needed to earn and the more money we earned, the more stuff we got. It was a vicious cycle of consumerism.

I noticed a shift inside my brain, at what I thought I knew – at my world view, so carefully managed and shaped by the country and culture I grew up in.

Looking at this man and his family, living in a classroom, with very little stuff, their generosity astonished me. This meal must have cost them a significant portion of that small income. But Dr Sòng shared not only his knowledge and interests with us, but brought us into the heart of his family, probably knowing we Americans would judge him and his country harshly. There was a strength of character in Dr Sòng that hadn't been broken by limits on his freedom or a low salary. I saw a man who valued his family like I did and valued his work like I did. We had that much in common, even if we lived in vastly different worlds.

That afternoon, Guy let us loose in a huge park to roam around. Hetty had a headache and went back to the hotel. Charon and I walked along together, splitting off from the others.

Everywhere we looked there was a group of about 50 people doing something together – mainly of retirement age. There were Tai Chi groups, sword groups, different kinds of dancing, singing, people playing ErHus and other instruments. I saw a group putting on a play, people painting together, doing martial arts. The variety of activities was astonishing.

'Retirement at 55,' Charon said, bitterly. 'I'll never be able to retire then.'

I nodded in sympathy. It didn't bear thinking about when you were a teacher. Retirement always seemed a long way off.

'Why don't we try to find something to eat around here? I'm hungry.' She turned to look about herself.

'In the park?' I said, 'Where will we find food?'

'Let's try going up that hill. At least we might have a better view and can spot a food truck or something.'

We walked along a path up a sloping hill.

'It's kind of sweet, all these old people. With their clubs,' she said.

'Yeah. And they do it all themselves. Did you notice? It's not like they get to go on cruises or anything. They just have this park and they entertain themselves.'

'It's a bit strange, no kids or young people.'

'But they're all playing like kids.'

'That's true. They look happy. Still in those groups of 50.'

I remembered the mannequins in the department store and our running for the bus when they all came crashing down.

We reached the top of the hill and found a food truck. But the menu did not entice me.

1. Pigeon on a stick. With feathers.

2. Roasted Chicken Feet.

3. Eyeballs. About the size of human eyeballs. In a yellow sauce.

4. A paper cup with fried bees in it.

'Still hungry?' asked Charon, brightly.

I struggled to decide which offering I could take.

Pointing to the fried bees, I felt determined to try them. I thought I'd been pretty adventurous already, having eaten boiled cow's hoofs, snake wine with a dead snake at the bottom of the bottle, and eel.

I put my money down and took up the chopsticks. Charon waited, watching my face. With rather improved skill at using chopsticks, I picked up one of the fried bees.

'I wonder if the stinger is still in it,' Charon said.

I put the bee in my mouth anyway, and chewed.

It was crunchy. Salty. Tangy.

'Hmmmm,' I said, trying to make her jealous. 'They must put some special spices in it.'

'Yeah, right,' she said and swatted my arm.

'No, really. Tastes like Ranch Chips,' I said, and took another bite. 'Want some?'

'No thanks.'

I finished them all and felt very proud of myself. We went back down the hill and came across a lovely sight.

About a hundred couples were dancing together to some American rock and roll music on a boom box. They were dancing the Swing. With gusto.

Charon and I laughed out loud. It was such an incongruous sight.

'They're pretty good!' cried Charon as we drew closer. I was impressed too. I took out my camera and started snapping pictures. Guy wasn't around to see me and I didn't care if he did anymore. These were expressions of utter happiness, people lost in the dance.

The boom box was belting out a new song with a strong rhythm and the couples were swinging with soulful energy. One couple turned when they saw us and waved. It was a friendly gesture but also one in which the irony was not missed. They pointed to us and then gestured at us to join them in the dance.

Charon grabbed my hand and dragged me over. We had danced this dance before. It was her favourite.

'We're doing this!' she yelled over the music and our bodies fell into line with all the others. We swing danced around each other and did the moves, knees bouncing in time with the music. Suddenly, we blended in with the whole group and without language, without interpreters, or rules, or barriers, we were with them, in the music, just dancing together, celebrating life. We were not so different, after all.

Dancing for over an hour, we all finally stopped when the music was switched off. Panting and gasping for air, I looked around and noted that these pensioners were astonishingly fit. No one was having a heart attack. They were tired but gleeful. Nodding to us, they clapped, as if we were their inspiration. We nodded back and clapped for them too. They had to be fifteen years older than we were, but we felt connected.

'We better get back to the hotel. Guy will be waiting,' Charon said.

'Right.'

As we walked, Charon slipped her arm through mine.

'That was fun.'

'Yeah, it was.' I thought about taking her arm away, but the good feeling I was having made me just leave it there. We walked out of the park, slowly, and by the time we got back to the hotel, I was wondering if Charon's mood might be softened enough to propose something.

I stopped at the foot of the steps.

'Why don't we just do the prudent thing and call this interview off? We could both get into a lot of trouble over it.'

Charon's serenity was broken. Her face turned ugly.

'Nice try. But I am having this interview, Grant. There's no way to stop it now. These women are coming a long way and they expect an interview. We're going to give it to them. They need this chance to speak as much as I need to hear them.'

'But listen—'

'No more arguing. I'll tell Guy about your pictures and you know what? I know your address. I could send a letter to your wife about how you seduced me in China, about the night we spent in your room.'

'What are you talking about? Come on, Charon! Why would you do that?'

'Because I can and I want this. So, here's the deal. I'm coming to your room at two o'clock tomorrow afternoon and you'd better be there.' She poked my chest with her index finger. 'You should be more afraid of me than the Chinese government.'

# Chapter Twelve

The next day, at exactly two o'clock in the afternoon, I was fingering the whistle in my pocket. Today seemed like a good day to carry an emergency whistle. There was a knock on my door. Room 39. I opened it and Charon stepped inside, closely followed by two Chinese women. I closed the door behind them.

One woman had grey hair, cropped short around her face. Her lips were clenched tight.

She was holding her gloved hands and her eyes were darting around the room, as if looking for cameras or listening devices. The other woman had thick eyebrows and long shiny black hair. She kept her eyes on Charon, her face cold as a stone.

'Lock the door,' Charon said by way of greeting. I could tell she was nervous. She carried a backpack and a cake box, which was odd, because Guy told us there was no such thing as cake in this part of China. It was unknown.

'Where did you get that?' I asked, nodding to the cake box.

'Across the street. A little bakery.'

'Really?'

'I got it for our guests. It has a Mickey Mouse on it,' she smiled with a kind of triumph, having found a cake with an American icon on it. She was wearing her false eyelashes. The eyelashes came out when she dressed up. It was part of her armour, like the rest of her heavy makeup. She set down the box and backpack and flipped her hair.

'Ladies, this is our guard for the afternoon.'
They bowed to me and I bowed back, ludicrously accepting my role as a nameless guardian.

'Do you ladies speak English?' I asked.

Both of them nodded.

'They worked for an English-speaking university. We have a mutual friend. Now. Help me set up.'

'How long do you think this will take?'

'No idea.'

I sighed. I could feel a rash developing on the back of my neck. A stress rash.

'You have another chair somewhere?' She asked. She had taken the only two in the room for the ladies to sit down.

'Nope.'

She sighed and pulled her video camera out and put it on the bed.

'I'll sit on the bed then. You stand by the door.'

I was happy to be out of the way and took my position.

'Why don't you cut the cake. Here's a knife.' Charon pulled a six-inch knife wrapped in a hand towel out of her bag, along with some paper plates and napkins. I could not see how this was a party situation, but I unboxed the cake. It had a crudely rendered Mickey Mouse on the top in coloured frosting.

'Cute,' I said.

Charon waved the knife, then flipped her hair again.

'Be nice, or you don't get cake.'

I took the knife from her and cut the tiny cake into four pieces and set them on the plates. Charon handed them out with the napkins.

'To our success!' She raised her plate and then indicated that we all dig in.

The ladies bowed but stared at the cake like it was worms.

'Come on, Grant. Bite into it. Show them how good it is.'

I shrugged and sank my teeth into the sponge cake, letting my taste buds get a load of what a Chinese cake was like. It was like biting into sawdust. That's when I remembered Guy saying there was no sugar in this part of China. No wheat flour. This was someone's idea of a cake. Someone with no experience of one.

'You wasted your money. It's awful.'

'Never mind,' she said. 'Let's begin. Go stand by the door.'

I set down the cake and went to the door just as someone knocked on it. Turning back to Charon, I saw she was as surprised as I was.

'Go see who it is!' she whispered, frantically, as she motioned for the women to follow her to the bathroom.

I opened the door a crack, my heart thumping.

A key girl stood there.

'You come down to lobby, please. Now.'

I was frozen with fear. This was it. The police would be down there and they'd take me away to a Chinese prison. I'd never see Katie or Ariel again. I struggled to find my voice.

'Who wants me?'

'Boss, he say you come. Now. Phone call.'

'Phone call?' My mind was racing. I closed the door and went to the bathroom where Charon had the door open a few inches.

'Who was it?'

'Key girl. Says her boss wants me in the lobby. Now. Phone call.'

'Phone call? That can't be.'

I shrugged. 'She's waiting.'

'Damn. You better go. Maybe it's nothing. I'm going to get started. You just keep cool. Don't panic. Take your time. Just listen and then hang up and come back and be quiet! We'll be recording. When you come back, if things are cool, just come in.'

'What if things are *not* cool?'

She screwed up her face.

'Then don't come back, you idiot! And for God's sake, don't bring the manager with you or anyone else. I'll be filming in here. When I'm done, I'll go back to my room and send these ladies back out to the lobby the way they came in. Remember. They came asking for you. For room 39.'

'Right.'

I was so anxious, I couldn't think properly. This could be it. Officials from the government telling me to prepare myself to be taken away for questioning. Should I find Guy? Would he even be on my side? He worked for the university. Oh, God.

Trembling, really shaking, I went down with the key girl to the stairs and the front lobby. The man at the desk, the manager, put the telephone in front me and handed me the receiver.

'Hello?' My voice was squeaky.

'Hi, Grant. It's your lawyer. Don't say my name. Just listen.'

My knees went loose in relief. I pulled myself together and tried not to show how happy I was to hear Katie's voice. My brilliant lawyer wife.

'Is the manager there listening?' she asked.

'Yep.'

'Can you get back into your room and get your camera, your wallet and your passport?'

'Yes.'

'Good. Get them. Then make a hasty exit from the hotel. Make sure no one is following you. Your job is to take pictures in Kunming because this is your last few hours in it. At five your time, take a taxi to the airport. Go to the British Airways counter and pick up your ticket to Gatwick. The portal is ready. You're coming home.'

She hung up.

I marvelled at my wife. She obviously got the message. She was getting me out. Now all I had to do was get my rucksack with just the essentials and leave.

Climbing back up the stairs, I tried to imagine the consequences for Charon. She was not going to be deterred from her goal. But no one knew what she was doing. She could finish her documentary footage without me. Once this was done, she'd be fine. She didn't really need me. These are the things I told myself, I just wasn't sure if I believed it.

When I got to room 39, the key girl let me in, and I stepped inside. In preparation for leaving tomorrow, I had put my most valuable things in my rucksack to carry on the plane. It had my wallet, passport, two cameras, my ErHu, and that book for Katie. The Mao lighter was in my pocket with the whistle. This was all I needed. As I slipped the rucksack over my shoulder, I could hear Charon interviewing.

'What was it like for you, during the cultural revolution?'

The old woman answered, her voice strained.

'We beat our teachers with sticks. We trashed the school and tore everything up. We went to live in the country...and grew our own food.'

Wow. I would have liked to hear more, but I had a plan and I was sticking to it. Making as little noise as possible, I stepped back out of the room and closed the door with a click. The key girl walked over and gave me a quizzical look, not quite understanding what I was up to, but I just smiled at her and used the Jedi mind trick. *Nothing is wrong here. The American is just going for a walk.*

I held the railing and went down the stairs, not rushing. Just going to get some air. Guy said we had free time. My shoulders were relaxed. I was going to enjoy every minute of the time I had left in Kunming – by myself. This was my chance, thanks to my genius wife, to take more pictures. Then I would be coming home.

As I left the building, a huge weight lifted from my shoulders. Freedom. At last. Now I could go where I wanted, see what I wanted. Alone. It felt like a huge luxury. So... American. I hopped into a taxi and asked to be taken to the centre of town. I held on, knowing it would be a wild ride. It was.

When we came to a screeching halt, I took a moment to pull myself back up on the seat, then paid the man and got out. Standing on a busy corner, I watched as people moved past me on the road, riding their bicycles – a river of people, all moving in the same direction. Wave after wave of them. Hundreds, if not thousands. All on black bicycles.

If all the black bicycles looked the same, I wondered how people didn't mix them up when they locked them up. Come to think of it, I didn't see many people locking them up. Why didn't they all get stolen? Guy said the crime rate here was very low. They still held public executions in the town square. Drug dealers. They shot them in the head. I suppose that deterred crime a bit.

As I stood there, pondering, a Chinese man and woman appeared, both wearing red cross arm bands. They walked toward me with purpose. I turned, wondering if they wanted someone behind me, but when I turned toward them again, it was clear these two were heading straight for me. They came up and each took me by an arm and started walking in the other direction, speaking rapidly in Chinese.

'Hey! What do you want? I don't speak Chinese! What's up?'

They just grinned and kept walking, taking me with them.

Maybe they're doctors, I reasoned. I was desperate to understand this. Or there's been an accident! They need blood! Did I look like a certain blood type? What on earth did they want with me?

Oh, GOD! This was it! I was being abducted! *Whistle! Whistle!* I struggled against their grip and fished out the whistle bringing it to my lips, but in my panic, I was hyperventilating and had no air left in my lungs to blow. Well. It had come to this. I was going to be sold into slavery. No one could save me now. I'd never see my family again. To think I was so close to escape, and now this! I started weeping.

'Chair massage!' cried the woman. 'We givva you good price! 10 Yuan!'

'Ohhhhhhhh!' I went limp with relief and they had to hold me up. Not a kidnapping. Oh, good. 'Yes. Yes.' I waved my hands and stood up on my own feet. 'Chair massage. 10 Yuan. Sure.'

They laughed and nodded like this was the most wonderful news. They took me around a corner and there was a green wooden stool. Next to it stood three other young masseurs. One young man looked like he might have been twelve. Just learning, I suppose. They sat me down on the stool and started in on my back and shoulders as two of the boys worked on my legs. One was using quite a lot of pressure and I cried out.

'Ow!'

Immediately, the older woman whacked him on the back of the head. He adjusted the pressure. Better. I sat back and enjoyed my massage, keeping my hand on my rucksack. When they stopped, I assumed it was over and started to stand to pay, but the woman pushed me back down. They weren't done yet.

A man with a long white beard was walking toward me. He was wearing a white doctor's coat. The old master, no doubt. I watched as he cracked his knuckles, then stepped behind me and started pressing down on my skull, massaging it with powerful hands.

My muscles immediately went loose as if I was a marionette and he'd cut the strings. I'd never felt so relaxed. After he was finished, I thanked him profusely. He bowed and accepted my 10 Yuan. I stood up, a new man. This...was...great! I asked him if I could take his picture and he allowed it. He stood tall and proud.

Strolling along the avenue, I revelled in my new body and in my freedom. I wasn't in the clutches of kidnappers, and I wasn't in Charon's power anymore either, nor confined to that group of teachers. No more schedules! No more buses. No more points for being late. I looked at my watch. I still had some time left.

There was an old man selling corn from a boiling kettle. I bought an ear to munch on. He slathered it with melted yak butter or some such thing. Then he added salt. Simple. Just what I wanted.

After sitting down on a bench, I enjoyed the corn as I watched the river of black bicycles go by again. Again, I wondered about the similarities and differences between American and Chinese cultures. What did these people riding by dream of? What if there was no choice about your job, if you could never travel, or could never have brothers or sisters? It was impossible for me to imagine how these people lived under all the restrictions imposed by the Chinese government. Yet, somehow, they did, and I had seen happiness, hope and generosity.

As if to jar me out of my thoughts, something happened. Everyone stopped their bicycles in the street, got off and ran like hell!

'What the—'

I looked all around and everyone was running for cover. What was this? Nuclear war??? And then it hit me in the face. Pelting, driving, stinging rain – coming sideways with a ferocious wind! It took me a moment to realise that this was a monsoon! It was knocking me down with the force of its impact, and I soon understood the urgent need for shelter. Everyone was ducking into any door or awning available and no one was barred. Everyone made room because we all needed protection from *this*.

I had squeezed into the doorway of a bookshop. The sound of the rain beating down on the ground, the trees, the roofs, was deafening. We all stood there watching in amazement at the power of nature to simply take over everything. Very soon the streets were turned into rushing water and then into rivers. Any parked cars were submerged or swept away. And no one was going anywhere.

I saw objects moving fast in the river that was the street. A bicycle, a tire, tiny chairs and tables, and then I understood. All those entrepreneurs had just lost their businesses! Now I saw the strangest sight of all. A huge ox was bellowing as it was pushed down the road by the growing force of the water. A man was desperately following it in a cart, waving a stick and having no luck in steering it to safety.

After about half an hour after this began, I wondered how I was going to get to the airport. But soon after, the sound grew less intense. The faucet of water went from full force to a lesser force and then, it became a trickle.

When this happened, a few people ventured out again with their bicycles, but I couldn't see where they could put them down. There were no roads anymore. All flooded. They carried their bicycles above their heads and waded into the brown water. I supposed they were trying to get home. What was I going to do?

I tried to ask the shopkeeper how long these things usually lasted, but he didn't speak English. Another man, however, with thick glasses, stepped over to me and introduced himself. He was a professor of Chemistry at Yunnan University. In answer to my question, he said, the monsoon had dumped a lot of water and it would be a while before order was restored. Some places would fare better than others, depending on their topography.

When I told him I had been with the group of teachers staying at the hotel, he shook his head.

'That area is probably flooded all right. You can't get anywhere near it now. Things might improve by tomorrow, but it's hard to say.'

'What about the airport? I'm actually supposed to catch a plane in three hours.'

'You shouldn't have any trouble getting to the airport. The roads are better and higher up than in the hotel area. But you should wait for at least another thirty minutes. It's chaotic on the roads right now.'

I nodded. He was probably right. As we watched the rain coming down, I had so many thoughts about my impressions of this country in the short time I had been here.

'Could I ask you a question on another topic entirely?'

'Certainly.'

'What's China's greatest challenge, do you think?'

He considered the question carefully and seemed to be taking stock of me. Maybe it was naïve of me, but I had the idea that being a professor, he might just be honest with me, give me his real opinion.

'Pollution,' he finally said. 'Our government is not treating polluting businesses with enough toughness and it's going to ruin us. Perhaps... *all* of us.'

I wasn't ready for so much truth. It was blunt, but real.

'Do you see a solution?'

'We have the largest population in the world. If our government doesn't take drastic action, no matter what other nations do, it won't be enough. The solution is to stop letting big businesses pollute. We have to reverse the process, not keep making it worse.'

I nodded.

'It seems your government will have to change policy then. Do you have hope that will happen?'

He smiled wearily.

'That's what I like about you Americans. Your hope. We have a proverb you may have heard of: Faith can move mountains. We've done impossible things before, because we've done them together. I hope not only our people can convince the government to change, but that yours can too. Every government has to change in this regard.'

It was an honest answer. This bookstore that shielded us from the rain, also shielded us from the limiting views of our countries. We shared a moment of just being two human beings concerned about the future of humanity.

# Chapter Thirteen

If I had had luggage, I would never have made my flight. But I didn't, so I did, if that makes sense. Twenty-two hours later, I had never been so happy in my life to arrive at my own doorstep, come through the front door, set down my bag and yell, 'I'm hoooooome!'

Ariel came bouncing down the stairs with Katie on her heels. They were both half asleep, but their arms were out and we had a group hug, dancing in a circle in the front room.

'Daddy, you made it back! You came through the portal!'

It was the middle of the night here.

'You didn't wait up for me???'

'We tried. We ate pizza and popcorn until we nearly burst. That usually works,' Katie said. 'But even Cassandra fell asleep.'

I turned to the old cat sitting on the table.

'Oh, Cassandra! How could you?'

Cassandra hissed at me. I had awakened her too.

'Come here, witchy woman!'

I drew Katie to me and kissed her with all the passion I possessed. She kissed back and we were going at it for a good minute, before we were tapped on the shoulder by Ariel.

'My turn!'

Katie stepped back gracefully and I grabbed Ariel and swung her around in a circle.

'Oh, my lovely lovely daughter! I missed you so much!'

'I missed you too, Daddy. It was a long time that you were gone!'

'It felt like a century!'

'Or a million years!'

'It was! The dinosaurs are gone! I didn't see any outside!'

She laughed and it was the sweetest sound in the world to me. I thought of Dr Sòng and how he watched his daughter dancing. I spun Ariel around in a circle.

'You know, I got to meet a little Chinese girl your age. Her name was Mae. She did a lovely dance. I took her picture. Would you like to see it?'

'Oh, yes! Did you take lots of pictures?'

'I did! Thanks to your Mum here. She saved me. Again.'

Katie laughed and pulled me into the kitchen. While I talked a million miles an hour, she put on the coffee, sliced some bread for the toaster, cracked some eggs and started breakfast.

# Chapter Fourteen

It was one month later and Ariel was playing the ErHu upstairs. Guy had been right about it being a difficult instrument to learn. It was screeching and groaning up there like a dying animal.

'Maybe we should try to find lessons for her,' Katie said, diplomatically.

'Where do we look for an ErHu teacher in St Ives?'

'I'll put up a postcard at the bulletin board in the bookshop.'

'Good idea.' I was being diplomatic too.

It was Katie, my love, my wife and my lawyer, who advised me to send Guy my official group photos so that I might be paid at least some part of the fee we agreed to. This I did and received a cordial email from Guy in response, along with payment of two-thirds of the agreed amount. Since I missed the week in Beijing, this seemed like a fair resolution to me.

I hadn't mentioned Charon in my email to him and he didn't mention her either. I tried emailing her when I thought she had returned to California, but got no reply. She was probably pissed at me for leaving without telling her.

'*Coward,*' hissed Cassandra with her mind. '*This will haunt you all your days.*'

It seemed to haunt me all right. I couldn't help wondering if anything bad had happened to her, if she got the footage she wanted for her documentary or if she gave it up. There wasn't anything I could do, however, so I kept busy.

I spent a lot of time with my boss, Leslie Stringer, who worked for the tourist board and got me most of my work as a photographer. She helped me edit my Chinese photos.

'These are wonderful, Grant! You've got to exhibit them,' she said.

I laughed.

'I'm serious. It could open up other work for you.'

'You telling me to get another job?'

'No, I can keep you busy all over Cornwall, but these are better than tourism photos. They're art. And you should show them.'

This surprised me. Art is what I dreamed of making with my photographs.

'I'll think about it.'

'Start local. But think about looking for more travel opportunities as a photographer. Maybe write some grant proposals.'

'There are grants for such things?'

She stared at me and then squinted in that way she has when she can hardly believe what she is hearing.

'I can get you a few leads.'

'Thanks. I'll look into that too.'

'Great. I'll always have work for you here, but it would it would be good for you to keep exploring other places with your camera. Good for your work here too.'

She smiled sweetly. Leslie was a business woman and I was very glad to be working for her.

The guys I play music with at *The Kettle and Wink* liked my China pictures. In fact, they got the owner to clear a wall for me to put on a one-man show. All the regulars at the pub came and gave me a thumbs up. These reviews were dear to me. Regular people in St Ives were looking at regular people in China and feeling a sense of connection. I liked that.

The customers at the pub wanted to hear about what I'd seen and heard in China. And the whole experience got me thinking about it more and more. I picked up some books in the library and started reading.

At a second-hand bookshop I found a book called *One Hundred Poems from the Chinese*. It was edited by a fellow named Kenneth Rexroth. I'm still reading the poems and the interesting information in the back about the poets who wrote them. Some were royalty, some were scholars, some were concubines. There were foot soldiers who wrote poems, and a Minister of War. One of my favourite poems was written by a man called Tu Fu, who lived out his later years on a houseboat and died in 770. As I was reading one of his verses again, my phone started buzzing. I pulled it out of my pocket, and saw it was Charon.

There she was with her hair up on top of her head, those eyebrows she drew in and thick eyelashes. My finger hovered over the button, but I couldn't press it. My phone started ringing louder.

'Your phone!' Katie cried from the kitchen.

Getting up from my chair in the reception room, I walked toward the front door as I hit the button and brought the phone to my ear.

'Hi, Charon! Ni Hao!' I said, as I stepped out the front door and closed it behind me. I moved as far away from my house as signal would allow and heard Charon's reply.

'Don't you Ni Hao *me,* you traitor.'

'Did you get back all right?'

'As if you cared!'

'Sure, I care. I've been emailing, but you never answered me. I was worrying – I mean wondering if you got your interviews and everything—'

Big sigh.

'As usual, we are not on the same page at all. I've been busy since I got back. Haven't gotten around to emails. For your information, I had to go on interviewing without you, which was very stressful! And, obviously, I am fine. In fact, I've never been finer. It's become clear to me that I do much BETTER without you.'

'Oh, I'm sure of that.'

'You missed Beijing, you ding dong.' As a teacher of high school students in a fancy school, Charon had adopted the habit of picking substitute words for swear words that couldn't possibly get her in trouble. I was returning to that habit myself with a six-year-old daughter around. 'The MacDonald's was pretty awesome in Beijing,' she continued. 'Their hamburger has sweet and sour sauce on it.'

'That sounds...*truly* awful.'

'It was fabulous! Especially after our food ordeal in Kunming. So, do you want to know what happened at the hotel or not?'

'Yes. Do tell.'

'Well...before the monsoon hit, I was interviewing away and Oh My God, that old woman remembered everything about the Cultural Revolution. She talked about how people were starving. There was a big famine, but she said it wasn't just the famine that caused all the deaths. She thought it was partly Mao's fault. Everyone left their jobs to join the revolution, but they were lousy farmers. They lost a lot of crops and they didn't know how to manufacture the food. Something like *30 million* people died of starvation. Her parents. Most of her family. No one could say anything against Mao or the communists. Not then. Not now. Not ever.'

'Wow. That's really something. Did you get it all on your camera?'

'I sure did. And then I interviewed the other lady, the one who had twins.'

'Right. What did she have to say?'

'I couldn't believe it. It was SO cruel. The poor woman couldn't help it if she had twins!'

'No, she couldn't.'

'It was insane. They made her divorce her husband so they could each have one child.'

'Not a great solution.'

'But rules are *rules* in China. They wouldn't make an exception for twins. Her husband moved out and they each got one kid.'

'Did they get to see each other?'

'The husband was given a transfer right after and he had to move far away. They aren't allowed to travel in the south, you know.'

'So sad.'

'Yeah.'

'What will you do with the interviews?'

'Well...big news.'

'Yes?'

'Really big.'

'I'm ready...'

'I'm getting married!'

This threw me. It took a moment for me to recover.

'Aren't you married already? To Todd with two Ds?'

She groaned.

'It wasn't a happy marriage, Grant.'

'I'm sorry. I don't recall you telling me that.'

'No, I didn't want to burden you with it.'

'Wow. So, when did you get divorced?'

'It hasn't happened yet. But it's going to. I moved out as soon as I got back, that's why I've been so busy. After the separation period is over, I'll be free to marry Guy.'

This threw me too.

'Hold on. Guy? As in Guy Anderson?'

'Yes. We're in love! Isn't that *amazing*?'

'It is. When did *this* happen?'

'Well, we'd been flirting for a while...'

I hadn't noticed any flirting, but maybe I missed it.

When did you decide to marry him?'

'Actually, he proposed in Beijing. This was after he found out about my documentary, the day you left. I think it was one of the key girls who told him. But I'm not a hundred percent sure. Doesn't matter. I'm not mad anymore, because he took it really well. He wanted to see the footage.'

'You showed it to him?'

'I had to. I was afraid he might take away my camera if I refused. Anyway, he liked it. And he even said he might be able to help with it. He had some excellent ideas. We spent a lot of time in his room going over it. We were stuck in the hotel anyway because of the flooding. And...well...one thing led to another.'

'Oh, my.'

'So, that's how we fell in love.'

'Gosh. That's...incredible. It...still seems kind of quick. Are you sure about the whole marriage thing?'

'OF COURSE, I'm sure! Guy is a very sensitive person. He *loves* me. He could see this was important and he wants to be sure we do it right.'

'We?'

'Well, yes. He's working on it with me now. He'll be my co-producer and he knows *everyone*. We can't show it in China, obviously, but when we have all the footage we need, we'll leave together and show it internationally. It will join other voices in protest of human rights violations in China.'

'Wow. And is this what you wanted?'

'Yes! I've always wanted to find the love of my life AND make a difference in the world and now I'll do both with this documentary!'

'Gee. Wow. That's...so great! But, uh, does this mean you'll move to China then, to marry Guy?'

'That's the plan, yes.'

'But you don't know the language.'

'What are you? My *mother*?'

'Sorry. Sorry. I guess you'll learn.'

'Guy is teaching me. I'm going to have the wonderful, exciting life I deserve, Grant. And Guy is getting me a job with him at the university teaching English, while we work on this documentary. I can meet more people to interview that way. It's perfect.'

'But, isn't that a bit dangerous? With how the Chinese government works and everything.'

'Guy has everything under control. He's going to look out for me. Like a real man.'

*Poor Guy.*

'Well, I wish you both the best of luck. I'd better get going.'

'Right. Well, Nee whatever. I just wanted you to know I was all right and that there are no hard feelings. I forgive you.'

'Good. Great. I'm glad. Take care, Charon.'

'You too, toots.'

Then she hung up.

When I got into the house and the shut the door, Katie was calling Ariel down for dinner.

'Everything all right?' she asked, when she saw me standing there staring at the young Chairman Mao lighter in my hand.

Before I could answer, Ariel came crashing down the stairs. Cassandra took up her place on the table, swishing her tail back and forth and casting disdainful glances my way.

I walked over to Katie and threw my arms around her, then kissed her.

'Daddy, are you going away again?' Ariel asked. The hairs on my neck stood on end.

'Maybe someday, but not for a long, long time.'

'There's no place like home, right?' She grinned and blinked at me. We'd watched *The Wizard of Oz* the night before, which felt oddly familiar.

'That's right, pumpkin. There's no place like home,' I said, as I kissed her on the forehead, and sat down to dinner.

This is a work of fiction, partly autobiographical, in which I used memories of a similar trip to China with art teachers in 1996.

The cover and illustrations for this book are reproductions of Chinese Propaganda posters. According to a blog post by Dr Amy Jane Barnes, who was asked by the British Library to determine copyright status of Chinese propaganda posters in their collection, such posters were intended to have wide circulation. However, in 1990 the Chinese government enacted copyright laws retroactively, which meant posters published on behalf of an organisation (the Chinese state, for example) would have copyrights until 50 years after the publication date. I selected only posters for use in this book that were published before the year 1971 to comply with this requirement.

Verification of the dates of these posters can be found here: https://chineseposters.net

The photo credit for the final image of the young Chairman Mao lighter is Axel Forrester. It is the lighter I got on that trip.

The design for the cover was done by Axel Forrester, using part of a Chinese propaganda poster for the state government dated 1968.

I will be sharing more posters and photos from this trip on Instagram. For more links and information, please visit:

www.axelforrester.com

You can find the first book in the Odyssey series, *A Cornish Odyssey* by Axel Forrester, and the audiobook, if you ask for it at your favourite bookshop, or you may find it on Amazon. My website has samples, coupons, more writing and information. Thanks for reading.

Axel Forrester

Here's what people are saying about *A Cornish Odyssey* by Axel Forrester:

'Funny and sweet. I loved it. Will look for more titles by this author.' Laura J. Conlon, UK. 5 stars

'Delightfully crafted.' Sea B., USA. 5 stars

'Uplifting and intriguing.' Amandastar, UK. 5 stars

'Charming self-discovery walk in deepest Cornwall.' Castaway, UK. 4 stars

ebook, paperback, hardback at bookstores and Amazon

audiobook narrated by Danny Horn

## Acknowledgements:

My thanks go to Stephen van Dulken, my husband, for his faith, love, support, and proofreading. Thanks to family and dear friends for their encouragement and to alpha readers of this story: Kathie Nielsen, Deirdre Gainor, and Cindy Baldassin. Thank you, Tanja Slijepčević, for your patient assistance. I appreciated the editing help of Jacqui Lofthouse and the folks at BooksGoSocial.

Thanks to readers everywhere, to supporters of my books, to independent bookstores and to the creative community in Hastings and St Leonards for the continuous flow of inspiration and connection.

Printed in Poland
by Amazon Fulfillment
Poland Sp. z o.o., Wrocław

12114747R00110